Boyd

II

D0463456

A Season of Mists

BOOKS BY HONOR TRACY

A Season of Mists
A Number of Things
The Prospects Are Pleasing
Silk Hats and No Breakfast
The Straight and Narrow Path
Mind You, I've Said Nothing!
Kakemono: A Sketchbook of Postwar Japan
The Deserters

A Season of Mists

a novel by

HONOR TRACY

Random House • *New York*

FIRST PRINTING

© Copyright, 1961, by Honor Tracy

All rights reserved under International and Pan-American Copyright
Conventions.
Library of Congress Catalog Card Number: 61-12144

Manufactured in the United States of America,
by H. Wolff

To Gamel Woolsey

A Season of Mists

One

"Terrifying," Ninian La Touche said to Miss Fellowe in a voice that made all but his sister Violet turn and look.

The two of them were perched on the stone balustrade round the terrace where Violet and the guests were at tea. It was a glorious afternoon in September. The sky above the rosy brick house was a deep blue, the terrace and the gardens under it were bathed in sunshine and the valley below lay in a warm yellow haze that hid the river from sight. Here and there trees swam up from this shimmering radiance and trembled as if dissolving. Doves cooed in their tower above the gabled roof and bees zigzagged from one flower to the next, drowsily, as if from force of habit.

And so, wondered Oliver Knox, what was terrifying Ninian La Touche? As a rule he picked his words as carefully as he did everything else. He was staring away from the Fellowe, away from them all, at something in the garden below, but there was nothing to stare at. Old McCardle the gardener was there, snipping the heads off fallen roses, and collecting dead leaves, and that was all.

Now Violet La Touche gave a gentle, a barely audible, cough. It reminded Oliver that she was speaking to him. It reminded him too, without exactly rubbing it in, that he was a lucky man to be spoken to by her. A mere Mr Someone rarely got into the La Touche circle even if he were rich; and Oliver lived on his wife. John Manley the historian, William Box the conductor, the nice man from *The Times* and Mary Taplin the painter—the other guests were more in the La Touche line: the La Touches were special people themselves and, in the nicest way, preferred everyone round them to be special too.

Oliver heard the cough and understood it, but he was not going to surrender. He was invited to Silverwood Court because of his marriage to Mary Taplin but he acknowledged the fact with only half of his mind. The other and dominant half led a febrile dance of its own, in which Mary's position was simply that of Mrs Oliver Knox and her renown mysteriously resulted therefrom. If anyone referred to her as "Mary Taplin" he would thoughtfully wrinkle his brows as if trying to think where he had heard the name; and when, as often happened, someone called him "Mr Taplin" his mouth puckered and his cheeks drew in as if he were sucking a lemon.

"Sorry, but I was curious to know what might be terrifying your brother," he said offhandedly, implying that this took a natural precedence over whatever she might have to say.

"Some business affair, shouldn't you think?" Violet's tone was a match for his. "What else would he discuss with a secretary?"

"Oh, is Miss Fellowe that? I thought she was still at school."

Violet raised her eyebrows very slightly. She found it impertinent of Oliver's thoughts to go running about the La Touche demesne. "She is not as young as she looks," she said.

"What terrifies you, Ninian?" Manley called out.

"The way the summer has flown." He got off the balustrade and came towards the others, walking a little stiffly, as if the stone had chilled him.

"I think it has gone very slowly," Miss Fellowe remarked.

Violet looked at the girl attentively, as if hearing her speak for the first time.

"And it's not nearly over," Mary Taplin cried. "The best of the year is still to come." She began eagerly spooning up and swallowing the wet sugar from her teacup.

"That's my dear Greedy Nan!" Ninian said, looking affectionately at her. He was a man in the late fifties but as thin as a boy. His hair was perfectly white, like his sister's, which somehow only added to the youthfulness of his face, a lean distinguished face with black eyes and a fine aquiline nose. Violet and he were remarkably alike, even to the sharp little frown that never left their foreheads even when they smiled.

Oliver Knox sniffed pointedly and when no one took notice of it cleared his throat for good measure.

"Snuff? Snuff?" John Manley suggested, offering an eighteenth-century snuffbox to the conductor, who raised a long white hand in refusal. "As a rule I only take snuff on Sunday," Manley went on, putting a pinch on his wrist. "But today feels very much like Sunday." A voluptuous look came over his face as he inhaled the spicy dust.

There was a roar in the sky and a silver monster of terrible aspect tore over the house: then came a bang like an exploding bomb and all the windows rattled. One or two leaves fluttered down from the roses on the wall.

"So much for Sunday," Violet said.

"The aerodrome is a hundred miles off and more," said Ninian ruefully. "But what are a hundred miles today? Well, has everyone finished? And shall we set off on our little tour?"

He had promised to show them a lake which had newly been made at the far end of his grounds. Nowadays to build an artificial lake and island, rather than a swimming pool with a lido and cocktail bar, might easily have appeared as precious, but Ninian could do these things successfully.

"You go ahead," said Manley, leaning back in his chair and closing his eyes.

Ninian and Violet exchanged a look, knowing too well what this portended. As soon as their backs were turned the eminent historian would be into the house, moving with a light agility amazing in one of his bulk, there to ingratiate himself with the Italian couple. Like all else at Silverwood Court the food and the waiting at table were outstanding, Olimpia Ricci taking charge of the one and Tito her husband attending to the other. They made an exemplary pair and were the envy of all who came to the house. John Manley's wicked design, freely admitted to his associates, was to lure them away into his own service. He was nothing like as wealthy as Ninian, nor did he live in comparable style, but he had a villa only eleven miles from Olimpia's birthplace where he spent a part of every year, and he spoke a beautiful Italian in which he shamelessly buttered her up. Thoughtful men had declared the chances about even.

"Oh, why don't you come?" Ninian asked reproachfully.

"Too old and too fat," Manley replied with his eyes shut.

"I'll stay here too, then," Violet said, settling back in her chair.

"No, please! You mustn't think of it," Manley exclaimed, opening his little eyes again. "I wouldn't spoil your pleasure for the world."

"I can see the lake at any time," Violet said.

"But the others would never forgive me. Do go!" Manley implored her. The thought of the others deprived of their Violet agitated him immensely. "I'll just have forty winks. I should love to have just forty winks. A sleepless night . . ."

"Forty winks will be delightful," Violet agreed, composing herself to rest.

"The omens are unpropitious, Manley," Ninian

put in with a chuckle, and the scholar rose sulkily to his feet.

"Come on, Mrs Knox," Oliver commanded Mary, who in fact was waiting.

Manley walked on ahead, a bear of a man in slovenly corduroys, defying the others to speak to him as if they had done something wrong. Then came William Box, waving his arms as he ran over a passage of the *Verklärte Nacht* in his mind. The man from *The Times* explained to Violet, who did not listen, why his paper found it necessary to take up a certain attitude to one of the day's problems. They were followed by Mary and Ninian, with Miss Fellowe and Oliver bringing up the rear.

McCardle was halfway across the bed of roses when the party came down the steps, leaving neatness and dullness behind him as he went.

"A glorious afternoon, McCardle," Ninian called out pleasantly.

"Ay. We'll pay for it, I shouldn't wonder." The gardener was stooping over a bush and did not look round.

"The roses keep up wonderfully, don't they?" Mary called.

"Nay. They're finishing early."

"How are the Porlock chrysanthemums coming on?" inquired Ninian, in reference to some very special plants that had been given to him by a famous grower.

At these words McCardle straightened up, his bony face transfigured. "I'm obliged to conclude," he reported, beaming, "that yon are a total failure." He returned to his work with a happy smile.

"I simply cannot bear that man," Ninian confided to Mary, although he seldom uttered strong opinions, "and he is not even a particularly good gardener. But nowadays what is one to do?"

He changed the subject and began to talk about the exhibition of her paintings that was to be held in London at the La Touche gallery. "We've booked you for early November," he said. "It's not on top of the summer holidays and not too near Christmas either."

"You're awfully kind to me, Ninian."

"Ah, we must cherish you: we don't make money out of the good painters as a rule," he teased her.

Little Miss Fellowe gave a cry. "It's nearly seven o'clock by the sundial," she exclaimed. "Surely that must be wrong?" And everyone laughed.

"You see, the sundial never heard of Summer Time," Oliver explained, very kindly, for the girl looked quite upset.

"But don't they put it back?" she asked without thinking, from the sheer confusion of being laughed at; and they all laughed at her again.

"My dear, if we could!" Ninian came and stood beside her, looking down at the sundial's face.

"Dear Billy, do give the orchestra a rest," Violet besought William Box. "They will complain to their union if you don't take care."

"Sorry, very r-rude of me," the conductor replied, desisting. "How n-nice the garden does look, Violet. What's that pretty fuf-fuf-fuf fuf-fuf-flower?"

"That is a dandelion, Billy."

"Oh, is it? They seem to do wow-wow-wow-well here." Now come on, first violins, he silently exhorted them, helping with his hands: an eloquent *sostenuto*, if you please.

"And so, what else could we have done?" resumed the man from *The Times*. "Without going the whole way and taking the Socialist position, I mean?"

"I do not know," Violet admitted. Had Ninian said "My dear, if we could" or "Oh, dear, if we could" just then? Not that it really made any odds but she wanted to be sure. She always wanted that: she kept the childhood's feeling for her twin that he had lost, and never been quite forgiven for losing.

"My own opinion exactly," the journalist crowed.

The small but delightful property of the La Touches lay between two larger ones that had both been acquired by the National Trust. Ninian had been able to construct his lake at the end of it without the fear of a change in ownership leading to disagreeable developments and undesirable neighbours. Water was plentiful, as springs abounded and a vigorous stream rose in the hill above and flowed down to the river; and for the rest, it had been achieved by his own taste and ingenuity, and the fanatical determination with which he had kept to it and driven his workmen on.

"We shall put shrubs there this autumn," he said, looking across at the island. At present it was bare except for a small white folly with a domed roof. "Purple rhododendrons, we thought."

Manley cheered up all at once, for he saw a way of getting his own back. "It's truly splendid, Ninian," he said. "How all this must make you wish you had an heir! I mean, a son," he amended, for there was always the detrimental sister's girl.

"Ninian does things for the love of doing them," Violet said, as her brother was silent. "Like all artists. What made you say that?"

"Beauty ought always to be passed on," Manley said, retreating.

"You haven't passed on yours," she said drily.

The allusion to his unfortunate appearance brought Manley's claws out again. "By the way, I stayed in the same house as your sister the week end before last," he said. "She arrived unexpectedly, such fun! I rather think she is still there."

Mrs Cloud was famous for the length and horror of her impromptu visits.

"You do get about," said Ninian, as Violet in her turn was bereft of speech. "I say, what on earth is that?"

The others could hear nothing and supposed he was merely trying to change the subject. But his ears were keener than theirs and in a few moments they too were wondering what the strange noise could be. It sounded, if the idea were not absurd, like a cinema organ and it came nearer. Then through the trees they caught sight of a figure, dressed in the uniform of its day with trousers narrow as a pipe, long loose jacket and pointed shoes. In one hand the youth carried a wireless set the size of a brick: the horrid din grew louder with every step he took, an offence to the beauty of his surroundings. He walked towards the party as if he had every right to be there.

"Good evening," Ninian said with a host's manner.

"Oh, hullo," the youth said without pausing. His hair grew to a peak on his forehead and under thick brows the eyes were bright and impudent. "Hullo, my lovely," he said to Miss Fellowe as he passed her.

"These are private grounds," Ninian exclaimed hotly, a thing he had never done when trespassers crossed his path before.

"So what?" the youth called out. He did not look back but tramped sturdily on, the wireless howling in his hand, towards the boundary wall.

"The new cave man," Manley said, thankful to see the hostility switch to someone else.

"Let us go in," Ninian said abruptly. "I daresay we should all like a drink."

The little encounter had made an unpleasant impression on all save Mary and William Box, busy in worlds of their own; or rather it left a different bad impression on each of the others. It reminded Violet once more that her brother was positively not himself today, that something really was up: it disappointed the nice journalist, who loved to see the wrongdoer put down, and irritated Manley who always wanted everyone but himself kept out of everywhere. Miss Fellowe suffered most, for she had taken his greeting as uttered sarcastically and, still tormented by having been laughed at, felt more stupid and coltish than ever. At the present time Miss Fellowe's world was either all black despair or all scintillating wildly with joy; and it would veer from one condition to the other for the lightest imaginable cause.

Having done with Schönberg, the mind of William Box now came dashing along after the conversation, picking up one by one the words mechanically recorded on it like a retriever following a scent. Presently, red with anger, he walked up to Manley. "You are an absolute shuh-shuh-shuh shuh-shun-shuh . . ." he exploded.

"Shit?" the historian suggested. There was something a little beguiling about his self-awareness. Box vigorously nodded his head.

"Come, come, that is excessive," Ninian objected, with a pleasant smile. As if to make up for it he devoted himself to Manley for the rest of the way to the house, giving him generous praise for a series of talks held on the Third Programme some time before and showing by what he said that he had not forgotten a point or missed a nuance.

"I'm sure you're very good," Manley said simply. He could be moved by generosity although himself incapable of it.

"But no, it is we who are indebted to you," Ninian replied. "I meant to write to you at the time, but you know how it is."

How kind he is, thought little Miss Fellowe. And what beautiful clothes he does wear. But does he think me a perfect fool? She looked with admiration at his worn face and silvery hair, and the cameo ring on his little finger.

It occurred to Oliver Knox that he had gone unnoticed too long and the minute they got to the house he set about remedying this. As Violet asked Mary what she would drink, "I am sorry," he said, "but we must go home." They lived in an ancient watermill, converted by Mary into a dwelling, on the banks of the river half a mile away. "I like to get in before dark," he said, as if the country were swarming with jaguars.

"Oh, surely not yet," Violet exclaimed. "We supposed that Mary would dine. Ninian hoped to settle a few things about the exhibition this evening. He'll drive her home, if you want to go."

"She has a number of things to do for me," Oliver said with an air of rebuke, as if to say that first things after all came first. "And she has been out rather a lot lately."

"But surely her work is more important than anything else," Violet said.

Oliver's mouth puckered up as he answered that, curiously enough, this was not at all the case: that, strange as it might seem in the present day and age, there still happened to be women who put their husbands before themselves. He spoke as if Mary were not there, or as if she were an animal, in a way that Violet found aggravating.

"Ninian, do you hear? Mary has to go," she said.

Ninian broke off a discussion with Tito about the drinks and looked at the artist fondly. "Ah, to be sure, la petite épouse orientale." He smiled. "I'll ring you up and we'll fix a time. It will be easier to talk alone."

"If it's urgent . . ." Oliver began.

"No, no, no." Ninian looked at him, courteously trying to remember who he was. "Goodbye for now, my dear." He kissed Mary, "I'll telephone in the morning. Reynolds has been inquiring for the advance notices."

"Goodbye, everyone," Oliver airily said and walked off without waiting for them to respond, as in any case they failed to do, while Mary followed at three paces like an African woman.

14

"Can you understand it?" Violet asked.

"These things are often mysterious," her brother replied. "So, Tito, sherry for Miss La Touche and . . . what shall Mercy have? Milk? Ginger beer?"

"May I have sherry too?" whispered the girl, melting with bliss at the use of her Christian name and the tone of friendly raillery.

". . . sherry for Miss Fellowe, Mr Manley and me, whisky and soda for Mr Wold."

"Sisignore." The little man moved daintily away and then turned, pirouetting and balancing like a butterfly. "Signore! The women-istituto telephone-a."

"Oh?" A look of annoyance came over La Touche's face. This crew of female pirates had nobbled him to give a talk in the parish hall on Braque. They were not in the faintest degree, he well knew, interested in Braque or in any other painter: they had not the remotest idea of what painting was but they were all out for something they called Culture and, in their horrifying way, were resolved to come down on any bearer of it foolish enough to reside within the spread of their claws. "What did they want, Tito?"

"Not know." Tito had but a poor opinion of *istituti*. "Telephone-a one-a two-a three-a time. I say, them, il Signore was go out."

The thought that struck Ninian now made him feel just a little ill. Turning to Miss Fellowe, he said: "My dear, when was the Braque affair to be?"

Miss Fellowe swam up out of her world of felicity, pondered a space and turned white to the lips.

"I expect you to remind me of things," he said plaintively, and she leaned back in her chair with closed eyes.

15

Violet watched the pair of them expectantly. Confusion, muddle, people inconvenienced or disappointed, all were things her brother disliked, and now through the heedlessness of a girl he had been guilty of them himself. It might be a lesson to him not to depart from normal ways. Advertising some weeks ago for a new secretary, he had stipulated as usual that her age was to be from twenty-five to thirty and that she must have had experience of similar work; and had then, if you please, engaged a chit of a thing fresh from her training school, a local establishment, with no experience at all. "Miss Fellowe is what I want," was the only explanation he would give. Violet made it a rule never to criticize Ninian, beyond occasionally looking at him in a certain manner, but she had thought it terribly rash. Was it not, too, a rather peculiar eighteen-year-old who would venture to answer the advertisement, who would so confidently offer her unqualified, incapable self? Such were the thoughts that went through Violet's mind as she waited for one of Ninian's rare bursts of temper.

But to her astonishment he only said, "Good heavens, child, it's not as bad as all that." Miss Fellowe continued to lie there, pale and with closed eyes, as if unconscious. "Mercy!" he said sharply, laying a hand on her arm. "Manley, open a window. Violet, what shall we do?"

"Nothing," said Miss La Touche. "It will pass of itself."

Miss Fellowe opened her big green eyes that focussed in an uncertain way, squinting a little now outwards, now inwards, like those of a kitten, and fixed them imploringly on her employer's face.

"You gave us all a severe fright," he said in smiling reproach.

Violet gently cleared her throat, dissociating herself from his statement. "It is probably a touch of indigestion," she said, for Miss Fellowe ate very well.

"I am most terribly sorry, Mr La Touche," she muttered, the world about her in ruins again.

"Forget about it," he told her. "I will go now and grovel to the ladies by telephone. With any luck at all, they will refuse to forgive me. Tito, Mr Wold and Mr Manley will dine."

"Sisignore," the little man said. He served them with drinks and tripped away to Olimpia below. "The old man is in love," he reported.

"Mamma mia!" and she clapped an enormous hand to a generous mouth. The gaiety inspired by the news led to a verve in cooking which in turn resulted in even her own standards being surpassed.

At dinner Violet gave her little set piece on the Italian character, how routine irked it but the unexpected, the emergency, stimulated: she gave it nowadays every time there were extra people to a meal and Olimpia had risen to the occasion, without noticing that she did so. Ninian thought that his sister was ageing very fast.

Two

Soon, very soon, Mrs Harte, Mrs Rearden and Miss Dugdale came to tea. After the fiasco of the institute lecture there had been nothing for it but to invite the leaders to the house. This was done but rarely, so rarely that Ninian could have remembered and counted each separate occasion, and yet, as he sat there and listened, he had an odd sense of its happening all the time. It seemed to him that a great part of his life was spent in hearing what a tomboy Mrs Harte had been as a child, and when she fell silent at last and Miss Dugdale took up, to describe a sunset she had marvelled at over the Bay of Naples, he felt he had lived through this very scene before. Not only her description but her way of looking over the shoulder of the person to whom she spoke, as if unable to bear the human eye, were familiar; but this sunset had occurred during a holiday from which she had only just come back.

". . . inspired in me feelings akin to awe," she concluded.

While she spoke the other two ladies had been glancing about them. The beautiful weather kept up but Violet had ordered tea in the library to discourage lingering. They had glanced with admiration at the tall silk-lined bookcases, at the Morisot and the Juan Gris, at the great marble bowl of scarlet dahlias; and at Ninian's throat with surprise. He wore no tie, although the dandyish summer suit he had on required one. The effect was of a negligence, even an absent-mindedness, that did not go with him. They kept looking at it and then up into his face, as if trying speechlessly to convey a hint of their disapproval while he, unheeding, smiled dazedly at Miss Dugdale.

"Quite so," he said now.

Violet offered her guests more tea, an invitation they knew better than to take at all seriously.

"And now," said Mrs Harte, with a coy look at her confederates, "shall we pop the question?"

Ninian steeled himself to meet it. He had known the penalties of conduct like his could not be light and he had rather allowed his imagination to run away with him. The women had been so kind! They fully realized how busy he was and how very easily —when they came to think of it, for of course they themselves had been counting the days—a small thing like the lecture could have slipped his mind, how generous indeed he was to have agreed at all when he had so many important *and much more interesting* affairs to think about. It had been, they feared, most presumptuous on their part to have approached him at all. Ninian had fairly, and justifiably, shaken in his shoes as they went purring on, but his wildest, most hysterical forebodings fell short of what Mrs Harte was now to propose, and that in the coolest manner. She began by saying that a party of them was going up to the French Impressionist Exhibition at the Royal Academy on Thursday next (cheap day-excursion), smirking at him with her head on one side as if no other explanation were needed and he must surely guess what they had in mind.

"Do you want me to talk to you first?" he asked. His heart sank at the idea, for there were in fact a great many things he ought to do.

"Well, no, actually." Mrs Harte looked roguishly at the others again. "Actually, we were wondering if we dared ask you to take us round."

"Round where?" he asked, bewildered.

"Round the exhibition, of course!"

He looked at her as if wondering if he had heard aright. "You mean, I should come up to London with you?"

"Or we could meet you there," Mrs Harte suggested.

"Isn't Professor Seligmann coming on Thursday?" Violet said at once. Ninian was not quick with little social lies, as she was, and he hated saying "no" to anyone: he was looking benignly at the impudent woman now.

"No," he replied. "I have no appointments on Thursday."

Have it your own way, she thought, vexed. As a rule he was grateful for the life lines she threw him.

"Then we are in luck," said Mrs Harte. "Good biz!" cried Mrs Rearden, and Miss Dugdale gleefully rubbed her hands.

"I will have no appointments on Thursday," Ninian repeated in a loud voice. All looked at him, surprised, Violet more so than any of them. He jumped boyishly to his feet, exclaiming, "Who's coming out? It's too fine a day to sit about indoors," although it had privately been agreed there should be no garden-viewing. "I want to show you my swing," he said to Mrs Rearden, who wore little bows of ribbon in her grizzled hair. Violet's amazement now mingled with consternation, for there was not, and never had been, any swing.

"How awf'lly jolly!" Mrs Rearden cried, clapping her gouty hands.

"Ah, I forgot. The swing has gone to be mended," Ninian sighed. "But come along, off with us."

Hardly were they out of the front door than the telephone rang and Violet turned back. Tito had answered by the time she got there.

"Was the Signora Cloud," he said with a broad smile. He and Olimpia, like most servants, adored the family terror.

"Oh." There was really no limit to Poppy's effrontery. Only the other day she had sent in another huge bill for long-playing records, gifts, as Ninian and Violet well knew, to the gigolo of the moment, and Ninian at last had determined to send it back. Poppy had been as well provided for at their father's death as he and Violet, and she had supplemented her means by four rich marriages, two of which had ended in widowhood and two in divorce. Ninian had inherited from various sources and had made money from pictures, but even so he was no wealthier than Poppy. Yet bills came pouring in, for records, villas in the south of France, suits for young men, made by fashionable tailors, antiques, the Lord knew what, but all highly unsuitable. Up till now Ninian had settled them, partly from brotherliness and partly because they were always final demands and he hated the thought of scandal; but the more he paid the more she expected, and at last, egged on by Violet, he had decided to call a halt.

"Is going to see *Fausto* this evening," Tito went on.

Faust! A likely story.

"Is sorry, cannot come to your cocktail party," he wound up.

"Thank you," Violet said.

There was no cocktail party. The La Touches did not give cocktail parties. At the most they had a few friends in for a glass of sherry. In fact they were going to do so a week from this very day, but there had been no idea of inviting Poppy Cloud. It came to Violet, her anger mounting, that John Manley in his toadish way must have told Poppy of their plans when he ran into her over that week-end. Luckily, he had got the date wrong and she had fish of her own to fry. But what absolute impertinence, Violet thought, and how like Poppy to telephone and call off an arrangement that had never been made! It was the old story of the Gurney blood. Mrs La Touche had died giving birth to the twins and Mr La Touche had soon afterwards married a Miss Gurney; and although Poppy looked more like their triplet than a younger half-sister, her wild behaviour was always believed by them to result from the liquid that ran in the former Miss Gurney's veins.

"Please call me to the telephone if the Signora rings again," she said to Tito, smiling in case he should notice anything.

"Sisignora," he replied, remarking below in the kitchen, "More trouble with la cara Poppy," and Olimpia looked up from the nuts she was pounding in a mortar and laughed.

Now Violet followed after the others. She went the way that visitors usually were taken, past the roses to the long herbaceous borders, but these were deserted. She hurried back and round the house to the lawn with the great cedars here and there and the copper beeches behind that and again found nothing and heard no voice. Surely Ninian would not have taken them round the vegetables? But she went to make certain and at last, over the stone wall bounding the kitchen garden, across a deep ravine full of briars and elder, she glimpsed the little party on a sloping meadow beyond. A kind of terror rose in her heart as she looked. It was not only that the distance they had covered in so short a time was great but that they were, every one of them, on all fours. The figures in their light-coloured garments and with the gentle evening sun upon them looked for all the world like grazing sheep: the effect created was of a charming pastoral simplicity but Violet felt that something was terribly wrong. Then Ninian got to his feet, encouraging the others forward with a sweep of his arm. Violet remembered that a part of this meadow was being fenced off to protect the little spruces they were going to plant there from the deer, and it must have been under the wire of this new fence, invisible from where she stood, that the visitors had been crawling. The realization only aggravated her fears. What on earth was her brother about, to harry even unwelcome guests like this? Such a pace as he was setting! The ladies were toiling up the slope behind him, who tripped lightly ahead and turned every now and again to urge them onward and upward with that same rude commanding gesture. Violet could see that Mrs Rearden's face was almost black. Another instant, and Miss Dugdale was down, had measured her length on the grass. Violet waited, frozen, her breathing stopped, to see what Ninian would do. He made no move whatever to help the fallen guest but remained where he was, angrily waving them all on like an Army instructor with troops obliged to carry out their practice within a limited time.

Violet turned away in distress and walked slowly back towards the lawn. She sank down on the wooden bench encircling one of the great cedars near its edge and waited. Presently Ninian's voice was heard and the party came up the path through the wood, still led by him, who appeared to be in tearing high spirits.

"You wouldn't, of course, remember Naples before the war," he was saying to Miss Dugdale, who looked more dead than alive.

Violet rose and went towards them, nervously smiling. "A glass of sherry . . ."

"I fear we must go," Mrs Harte replied, smiling bravely back but with her eyes fixed in longing on the battered Morris Minor that had brought them all. The little car looked odd, standing there before the massive stairway of ancient stone that led up to the front door. Mrs Rearden sang as she breathed, like a kettle approaching the boil. "We shall so look forward to Thursday," Mrs Harte concluded as she prepared to drive them away. It was clear from her voice that the arrangement with Ninian still seemed to her worth the terrible walk.

"I'm sure, I'm sure," Ninian said, with the over-heartiness of a man who is not attending.

"We will get in touch again beforehand."

"Do, do."

"And thank you."

"Thank *you*."

They departed.

"Thank goodness for that," Ninian said. "I'm at the limit of my endurance."

"They are looking a little the worse for wear themselves."

"Oh, that was nothing! Do them good," her brother replied. "It's the chatter I can't stand."

"Then why let yourself in for a whole afternoon of it?"

He looked blankly at her. "My dear girl! What can you mean?" Then the blank expression turned to one of amazement. "You didn't suppose, did you, that I would take those hags round the exhibition?"

" 'Hags,' Ninian?" she echoed. All the ladies in

question were junior to them. And coarse expressions were new from her brother. She had a feeling almost as if the known familiar world were collapsing round her; and as if to rub it in, at that moment one of the terrible silver birds of prey screamed through the air over their heads and banged. Trying to speak composedly she went on, "I'm afraid you certainly have left them under the impression . . ."

"I think I want a nap," he interrupted, not rudely but as if she had not been talking. "I shall go and sleep for a while."

Without another word he went and lay in a hammock tied between two of the copper beeches. He looked up into the dense rosy foliage overhead and wished that tomorrow would come. Mercy had asked for the afternoon off. Presently he dozed and dreamed of Oxford. He was lying in a punt moored to a post on the bank and these moorings came away, his punt drifted down the narrow Cherwell and out into the river, it sailed helplessly and with gathering speed along in midcurrent, the banks on either side were crowded with yelling undergraduates who had eyes only for him in his runaway craft; motorboats continually put out from the jetties to save him, chugged up to his punt and turned and chugged away just as they came within reach of it. And he awoke all at once, for somebody was shaking him.

"Well? Well?" he muttered. How strange, he thought, he had been asleep and now was awake and yet the motorboat part of his dream still went on, the air was full of the humming of engines. . . .

"Oh, Ninian, they have come! They are here," said Violet's agitated voice.

"Who are?" he asked.

"All those we asked to sherry next week," she said. "Can't you hear them driving up? The Hartleys, the Drages, the Admiral, Mary . . ."

"How dare they?" he exclaimed, all but falling from the hammock as he jerked himself upright. "How utterly inconsiderate! I am surprised at Mary . . ."

"Ninian, it is a *mistake,*" Violet cried. "It is your Miss Fellowe, who put the wrong date on the invitations. Nothing is ready. Olimpia is in hysterics, you know how good she always is but she was making lasagne for tonight, so complicated, we have to send to London for the nuts. . . . Oh, do come!"

Ninian rapidly buttoned his shirt to the neck, fished out his tie from a pocket and put it on, and walked towards the house. "Violet, this is the last time we entertain." He spoke gravely, even pompously, like a man aggrieved beyond endurance; and yet somewhere deep within him a wild hilarity was bubbling. If they came today he would be spared their coming next week. He saw Mercy now as a kitten, snarling delicate machinery with deft, irresponsible paw, imagined green eyes wavering, pointed pink tongue appearing as same paw deftly guided pen over invitation cards. . . . Why, she had saved him too from having to address those fearful women on Braque——

"Telephone-a again, la Signora," Tito shrieked at them from the top of the steps. "Now can come after all, but later maybe." He was trembling like a leaf. Having given the message he dashed away to the interior.

"Who? What Signora?" Ninian demanded, leaping the stone steps two by two.

"Poppy!" Violet panted after him. "John Manley must have . . ."

"Poppy, here? Over my dead body!" He tore into the house and across the hall, passing without a word or a look two startled newcomers, streaked up the stairs and into his study. He ran to the telephone and snatched it up: with any luck she would not have left home yet.

"Silverwood?" asked a voice that he vaguely recognized.

"No, sorry," he said and put the receiver down an instant.

"Is that Mr La Touche?" said the voice querulously when he took it up again.

"No, no, no, wrong number," Ninian said, rattling the rest furiously. He could hear the voice stuttering through it all for a bit, and then it went off. "Exchange! Exchange!" He gave Poppy's number in Chelsea, drumming with his fingers on his knee and scowling out of the window. A burst of laughter came from the guests below. "Poppy, what does your message mean?" he snapped when at last she answered. Latin American music could be heard in the background.

"Can't make it, not my fault," came in the cheerful tones. "I'll be with you for dinner or bust, however. First invitation for twenty years!"

"Poppy, there has been no invitation."

"Don't be silly. It's here in front of my nose: very formal too, requests pleasure of, etc. Ow!" There was a sudden piercing yell. "Guy, that wasn't very nice."

Further noises mingled confusedly with the rumba. "See you at dinner," Poppy concluded, hiccoughing, and hung up.

"Outrageous!" Ninian spoke aloud to the empty room. He sat there in bewilderment, vaguely aware of the chatter of voices in the drawing room. Mercy must have sent the invitation off with the others, but why? He clearly remembered telling her to get Poppy's address from the book, type out an envelope to her, enclose the bill for the records together with the note he himself had written and send it off. It was the child's lack of experience, for the time being he would have to check everything she did. Still, why had she taken it on herself to— His eye now fell on a pink paper in the wire tray for incoming correspondence. It looked familiar. Apprehensively he seized it. It was indeed the bill, the final demand before proceedings began, for the long-playing records and attached to it was his own note and another: "Dear Ninian, I do see that you cannot any longer be responsible for my follies and absurdities! And Bill quite agrees. But this happens not to be one of them and we think you perhaps had better have the docket back again. Ever, Topsy Stroude." Ninian gave a groan. Bill and Topsy Stroude, two of the most inveterate gossips in London! But, at the same time, so valuable as a couple-about-town. It was Mary's *curriculum vitae* and a careful description of her new exhibition that had been intended for Topsy, who was then to go bugling Mary's name at all her parties. Topsy Stroude, Poppy Cloud, of course, the child had mixed them up, hadn't even been paying attention very likely. This was really too much, they couldn't go on in this way, he could vividly imagine the story Topsy was putting about. No, it was too bad.

Suddenly he was shaking with silent laughter from head to foot, wild lovely voluptuous laughter such as he had not known for many a long year. Within him sat his real self, if it was his real self, cool, censorious, making baleful little comments. I'm so glad you're amused, real self said, folding its arms. Its head shook a little from the force of its indignation. Frightfully funny, isn't it? And decent old Topsy will never say anything. I'm fond of a joke myself. . . . Ninian buried his face in his hands and gave himself up to the pleasure of it.

Violet hurried into the room. "Olimpia has locked herself in the cellar," she cried. "Ninian, what is it?"

"Nothing at all," his real self said, firmly taking control. "But I have consented to Poppy coming. We must make ourselves clear once and for all."

"Tonight of all nights!"

"She says it is her first invitation here for twenty years."

"When did she ever wait to be asked anywhere? Ninian," Violet said earnestly, "please will you join us? People are beginning to wonder. And I very much fear that the Admiral was drinking before he came."

"All right," he said, and Violet bustled away. Still he did not move. He sat there smiling and looking across the sunlit garden and down to the river threading its way through the poplar and willow trees that fringed the banks. The hum of conversation below was louder now, not so subdued, the guests were relaxing and enjoying themselves, and behind this hum he now and again caught the sound, faraway yet still penetrating, of Olimpia's voice as it rose and fell. Guests on the wrong day, cook in cellar, horrifying new secretary . . . there was a marvellous feeling of life in the house. And, he suddenly thought, it was life that had always been missing there. Taste, dignity, peace, contentment, everything had been theirs except life. Violet would not have approved of it and he had not really missed it! Yet here he sat with it surging about him and enjoyed the novelty with all his heart.

"Mai, mai, mai!" he heard Olimpia screaming.

Violet flew into the room looking pale and distraught. "Ninian!" she quavered, "John Manley is in the cellar too."

"No!" Her words seemed to release a spring in him: he leaped from his chair and bounded off, down the stairway, sweeping a glass of sherry from the hands of Miss Agnes Frobisher as she stood to get a better look at the *Pythoness, Drinking* ("I wouldn't want to *live* with it," she said ever after), by Isolowolotumba, and through the swing doors across the stone flags to the heavy studded door brought specially from Córdoba that closed the mouth of the cellar. "John, you thorough-paced scoundrel!" he shouted, hammering on this. "Come out directly!"

"My good Ninian." Manley's voice in contrast to Olimpia's came but faintly through the old Spanish timber. "I am afraid you are not yourself."

Olimpia was shrieking that she would bring witnesses to establish something or other.

"I see through this contemptible manoeuvre," Ninian replied, hammering again, furious and at the same time in the oddest way jubilant. "Come out at once or you leave the house for good."

"If I go," the muffled tones came back, "I fancy Olimpia will come with me. She believes that Violet has attacked her character."

"Manley: will you comply with my wishes or not?"

"I am trying to help you, La Touche."

"Liar!"

It was not, he realized at once, the thing to say to an historian. The great door swung slowly back and John Manley stepped forth. His little dark eyes in a face always pudgy and now white with anger were like burnt currants in a ball of dough. Before he could speak, however, Tito appeared from the other direction and began to pour out a stream of endearments in Italian. Accustomed to and proud of Olimpia's tempestuous outbreaks, he had finished what he was doing in the house before coming to see what she was at, well knowing that behind the cries and accusations and hysterical pleas to heaven to allow her to die at once rather than linger on unwanted and despised was simple pain at the guests having to go without the delicious little *amuse gueules* that she baked for them as a rule, combined with an artist's fury over the interruption to her *lasagne*. Hearing his voice the great creature at once flew out of the cellar and into his arms: the tiny man led her away still cooing words of honey. Manley opened his mouth again, to bring Ninian to his senses with a few searing remarks. For once he had been unjustly accused: he had in fact gone into the cellar merely to try and calm Olimpia down. He had rather enjoyed being locked in darkness with her, it was true, but his plan of enticing her away from Silverwood altogether had for some reason not been in his mind.

"It is rare on the whole in civilized communities," he began, but Ninian's thoughts had taken a new turning. Pensively rubbing his hands, he asked: "If you had your life again how would you live it?"

Manley grew angrier still. "As I have, Ninian, as I have. If I may say so, it is rare on the whole . . ."

"No, really?" Ninian appeared to be both interested and amused.

"Pray, is it normal usage in civ—"

"Never mind all that, put it aside," Ninian urged. "So you would do it all again. But I wonder if you would really."

"You sound as if I were in my dotage," Manley grumbled, giving up. He had always been annoyed by La Touche's habit of treating him as coeval when he was the younger by thirteen years.

"Tomorrow we die," Ninian blithely proclaimed, as if indeed that were the date fixed for it. From far off beyond the green baize came a crash, accompanied by the sound of breaking glass and of voices raised in alarm, to signify that the Admiral's legs at last had given way. Now a look of profound melancholy came into La Touche's face.

"And this evening Poppy comes here to dine," he added, in little more than a whisper, as he slowly walked away.

Three

The explanation that Miss Fellowe gave for her short-comings was a satisfactory one. She was, quite simply, terrified of losing her job. It was not just that she was poor and had a widowed mother, but also that the situation was so brilliant in itself and she had come by it in such a fairy-tale kind of way. Fear that her luck might not hold, anxiety lest her ability prove unequal to the demands made on it, confused her brain and all but wiped out her memory. Could her errors be overlooked this once, she pleaded, in a faint voice, while her green eyes struggled vainly to focus.

Ninian was moved by her admissions and pleased with her frankness. He had insisted to Violet over and over again that there must be a reason for what had happened. It was impossible, he now saw, that the girl should do good work in this state of tension. She had, it was true, let them in for a dreadful experience. Poppy had brought the lover called Guy, a pale smooth young man whose eyes sneaked and darted about the room at lizard speed, noting and pricing all that was in it. She was so tipsy that she had painted her lips askew like those of a clown: the effect, on her La Touche features, was to make Ninian and Violet feel they were confronted with some debasing caricature of themselves. Scabrous anecdotes and intimate asides to Guy poured from her lips all through dinner, and she drove off immediately afterwards, so that there had been no opportunity for the frank talk that Ninian was resolved on. Violet had been in a cold fury and referred more than once to Miss Fellowe as "that girl."

How fresh and young and simple she is! Ninian thought now. "But am I such an ogre?" he asked her, smiling.

"No, not really," she faltered. "It's only that you are so . . . you are so . . . It's all *me*," she concluded on a dying note.

"Let me test you," he said, to put her at her ease, holding up the reproduction of a painting. "Tell me, whom is this by?"

Little Miss Fellowe fairly quivered with apprehension. She had no idea at all. She saw that the painting was "modern"—further than that she was unable to go. The only "modern" painters she could, at times, distinguish were Van Gogh and Gauguin.

In despair she uttered the first name that entered her head, one that she had seen in a journal recently. "Dufy?"

"Bravo, my dear!" he exclaimed, looking at her with interest, even excitement. "Or do you know the picture?"

"No," Miss Fellowe honestly replied.

"Then you must have a very true eye indeed," he told her, "because this is not at all in his usual idiom. Ah, Mercy, anyone can be accurate and efficient but a true eye is a gift from the gods."

To her relief he did not test this gift any further but applied himself to the morning's post. He dictated some letters and, while she typed them, composed and wrote by hand an amusing letter to Topsy Stroude about the little muddle over the bill for the records. He read it aloud as soon as he had finished and they both laughed merrily.

Perhaps I shall be a success after all, Miss Fellowe thought, reviving.

Ninian's mind kept harking back to the matter of the Dufy, for he had known critics and art historians puzzled by that picture at first view.

"I do wish you would listen," Violet said. The wonderful weather kept up and they were having their coffee in sunshine on the terrace after lunch.

"What will you do about Mrs Bentley?"

Mrs Bentley was a rich and powerful county lady who supplied them, as a concession, with her marvellous cream and butter and eggs.

"What about Mrs Bentley?"

"I have been telling you. Ninian, do please attend," Violet said. "Mrs Bentley rang up here yesterday and you slammed the receiver down."

Ninian sat bolt upright. "What utter nonsense!"

"She insisted. She gave chapter and verse. It was about a quarter to seven last night. You answered, she recognized your voice, you said she had the wrong number and slammed the receiver down. Then you lifted it and waggled it about until she cleared the line."

"Ah, yes, yes," Ninian said, relaxing. "It comes back."

"You mean," his sister panted, "that it's true?"

"Something of the sort, I believe." He stared into the gold and silver haze above the river. He would never have been able to pick out that Dufy at eighteen, never. His eye was good, as good as anyone's, but it was a trained eye. How superior the natural gift always is to an acquired one. . . .

"Ninian, she is raging."

"Then let us ask her to tea."

"Mrs Bentley is not to be mollified by invitations to tea. She is not Mrs Harte or Miss Dugdale. She gets telegrams from the Queen," Violet explained. "You will have to do, oh, much better than that."

"I will send her a wire and sign it 'Elizabeth R,' " he proposed.

Violet looked at him and went into the house, returning almost immediately.

"McCardle is at the door," she reported. "He says, what is he to do with the deodars?"

"Deodars? Violet," Ninian earnestly said, "do let me have a little peace, like a dear woman."

"Two enormous deodars have arrived by rail,"

Violet told him. "McCardle is very much annoyed. He says they will not grow here at all and, also, that they will grow to a hundred and thirty feet."

How cranky everyone was getting, how odd and small and silly! There seemed a continual fuss going on about nothing nowadays. Or had it been like that all the time and he had never noticed? "Are they a present from someone?" he asked, trying to take an interest.

"You ordered them from Fawcett's," Violet replied. She was flagging visibly. "There's a note to apologize for the cost, and explaining that the trees were very difficult to procure."

"I? From Fawcett? No such thing." Now he felt angry, really angry, with the firm for their mistake, with McCardle for criticizing what he did even though he hadn't done it, with Mrs Bentley for telephoning, with Violet for going into things so laboriously, with everyone except . . . And then a thought came to him and his face brightened. "Ah," he exclaimed in joy, "it's our Mercy again!"

"Miss Fellowe?" asked Violet balefully.

"I remember telling her to order a pair of secateurs the first day she was here," Ninian said, laughing, "and so very naturally she orders a couple of deodars. Yes, that will be it. What a truly delicious mind, Violet! An Edward Lear sort of mind."

"Indeed! If Miss Parsons had done it . . ."

Miss Parsons was the predecessor of Miss Fellowe, a clean-limbed open-air girl who had left her post to make some highly suitable marriage.

"Mercy is an artist, not a machine," Ninian said.

38

looking away over the misty valley. "Do you know that she recognized a Dufy that experienced dealers and art historians have been unable to place?"

Violet retired into the house, and to her bedroom: it was her practice when discomposed to commune there with her three Siamese cats. Ninian got up, stretched and walked with vigorous steps in search of McCardle, whom he found standing between and dwarfed by the young cedars. The gardener's eyes were tightly shut and he moved his hands in the air as if hauling on a rope. The La Touches often talked about this habit of his, speculating as to what it could possibly mean. It was quite unlike any of the various compulsive acts their friends indulged in. Violet thought there might be a suppressed or unconscious desire to be a bell-ringer in church. The truth was really simpler: McCardle was hanging his employer from the limb of an imaginary tree.

He now placed one foot against the invisible trunk to get a better purchase on the rope and hauled away for dear life, hissing like a groom the while.

"Now then, Macmillan," said Ninian with severity. In moments of vexation he would often confuse the gardener with the porter at the gallery.

"Macmillan, forbye!" McCardle said, straightening his stiff back and glowering round at the speaker. Mixing me up with a Tory Prime Minister, he thought indignantly. "Did the sister gave you my message?"

"Do not refer to Miss La Touche in that manner, please," Ninian said. "And, McCardle, once and for all, if you wish to stay with me you must do your work without argument. Those deodars are to go in this afternoon, one each side of the entrance to the wood."

McCardle stared in amazement at the being whom he regarded solely as a wage-paying installation. "You should have spoken to me before ordering," he complained. "It's no' a rational concept."

"I will plant deodars from here as far as the eye can see, if I choose," Ninian assured him.

"It's murder!" McCardle cried. "We hav'na the soil nor the sun." But, unaccustomed to mutiny and uncertain how to deal with it, he weakened.

"Put them in," Ninian commanded, "and leave the rest to Nature."

At this the gardener rallied. "Nature!" he said, with vehemence. "Nature is daft. I sairtainly s'all leave nothing to a loon like Nature."

"McCardle, please!" Ninian turned on his heel and marched away to inspect the site for the deodars. The gardener shouted a request for ropes, pulleys, scaffolding, cart horses and a bulldozer at his retreating back and then fell silent. Stealing a backward glance as he turned the corner, Ninian saw him, one foot in the air, again pull on that invisible cord.

The wood was as English as could be, composed of beech, oak and chestnut, carpeted in spring with primrose and bluebell and surrounded by a hedge of briar and honeysuckle. How piquant, how unexpected, Ninian thought, would the two great Indian trees appear, standing up like the guardians of a temple! It was a touch that by himself he would never have thought of. As he stood looking at the pleasant scene before him the strange wild exhilaration of recent days swept over him anew. Misguided by the weather, a pink horse chestnut was vaguely trying to flower a second time: it reminded him of McCardle's comment on Nature, which struck him all at once as both delicious and profound. Gaily he walked on into the wood, out of the warmth and brightness into the cool dark, slowing down until his eyes became accustomed to it.

He was greatly put out by what he next saw. A little way ahead was a clearing where two or three trees had come down and in the middle of this, seated on a log in the sun, was a man. He had impudently lit a fire and as Ninian halted, wondering what to do, the smell of frying reached his nose. The intruder's back was turned but Ninian recognized him directly as the youth with the wireless, who had trespassed there before. Calmly he sat and fried his meal in the La Touche wood! Yet the proprietor felt an odd reluctance to intervene. He was much inclined to turn on his heel and walk away: he was afraid, certainly not of the fellow himself, for he was no coward, but of something happening to change his mood. But now the youth paused in his frying to turn the wireless on and the quiet wood rang with the notes of a popular soprano. If there was one thing Ninian could not abide it was a bad soprano and he always declared that if Violet's Siamese cats could sing, such would be the sounds they would emit; and he strode forward with an angry determination.

"What is the meaning of this?" he demanded. "Kindly put that fire out at once."

The youth looked round with the bright insolent eyes that Ninian remembered. "How'm I to fry the bangers, then?" he asked.

"You must take them elsewhere." Ninian walked round the log and stood facing him across the fire. A newspaper was spread on the ground, with bread, mustard, beer and a dirty comb on it. "This is private property, as I told you once before," Ninian went on. "You have no business to picnic on it."

"I like it here." Tenderly the youth rolled the sausages about in the pan. "You selfish old buzzard!" He grinned up at the landowner, his small pointed teeth, low forehead and shining eyes giving his face a wolfish look.

A growling began overhead and very slowly a squadron of silver monsters passed, flying immensely high. These and the mewings of the radio combined with the grinning lout's presence to awaken in Ninian a feeling almost of terror, as if he were looking upon the shape of hideous things to come. With this terror there strangely mingled something else that was not far from guilt: intuitively he sensed that the apeman crouching there was in a way his logical heir, the *reductio* of his own enlightened scepticism and refined irony, his refusals. With these ideas fluttering about in his mind he stood, civilized man confronting savage, timid and nonplussed and quite unable to think what to do.

All at once the grin vanished from the intruder's face. "Poppy told me any friend of hers was welcome here," he complained.

The words fell pleasantly on Ninian's ears. For the first time in his life he really was glad to hear of an

42

outrage perpetrated by his younger sister. Stripped of mystery, merely one more of her dreadful hangers-on, the youth was no longer a portent. "Mrs. Cloud did not tell me you were coming," he said.

"Mrs Cloud, is that Poppy, then?" the youth inquired. "She's a smasher, Poppy is. You're Ninian, aren't you? I didn't speak the other day, you with company and all. I'm Leo Piper," he revealed, on a note of triumph.

"And where are you staying, Mr Piper?" Ninian asked politely.

"I got a caravan down by the river," Mr Piper said. "Communing with nature, see? Doris gave it to me. Doris is another of my girl friends, like Poppy is. Doris and Poppy pick 'em young. I'm easy, long as they take care of me. I'm Poppy's youngest but one. Actually, though, I'm sweet on Isabel."

"Isabel is going to be a nun," said Ninian. His feeling of relief was wearing off.

"Poppy's daughter, a nun? That's rich," Mr Piper cried with a shout of amusement. "Things run in families."

"I'm surprised that Mrs Cloud did not tell you these grounds are patrolled by mastiffs," Ninian went on, as if Mr Piper had not spoken. "Happily, they are shut up at the moment."

"Mastiffs? Go on," Mr Piper cried.

"Yes," Ninian said, "we are neighbours, practically, of one of the new prisons-without-bars, you know. Something had to be done, we hadn't an egg or an apple," he improvised. "What the convicts left us the warders took. The mastiffs were a happy idea of the police."

43

"Police!" shouted Mr Piper. Hastily he began to collect his belongings. "I'm off," he said. "I won't half give Poppy what for, though. She never told me nothing about mastiffs. She said you'd be delighted to see me, and give me hot meals in wet weather. Said you'd always have a change of clothing for me. Women! I'll mastiff her." He shook his sausages on to a piece of newspaper and rolled them up, placed the bundle together with his other belongings in a filthy knapsack and set off at a smart pace without another word or a backward glance. Smiling, Ninian beat out the fire and scattered the ashes.

It was twenty minutes to four. He turned back and made for the house, thinking it was about time to go and see if Mercy had finished his letters. He pictured her there in the study by the open window, her hard young hands, brown after the long summer and childishly scratched, above the keys: typing, heaven knew what, ordering a chain of elephants, or a number of grand pianos to go here and there about the house: looking solemnly down at her work with those eyes, those big strange uncertain eyes that, nevertheless, could without hesitation pick out an unusual Dufy.

At the edge of the wood he stopped and fell to dreaming. There was no sign as yet of McCardle and the deodars, although confused shouts and bangings and scrapings were coming from the barn. Probably the gardener was assembling his gear and staff for the planting which, in truth, would be no small matter. Again, he imagined the two cedars in their place as mighty tutelars of the wood. But, he wondered all at once, how fast do deodars grow? And his stomach seemed to rise within him and turn over and over until he was left faint and dizzy. He looked away up the slope to the house and gardens of Silverwood, tranquil in the sun. A bough of late honeysuckle swung out from the hedge in front of him, framing the scene with blossom as in some carefully arranged photograph. Now he stared upwards, into the hot unending blue of the sky, and once again there was the horrid turmoil within.

Surgit amari aliquid . . . the words bobbed up in his mind, but there was no *aliquid* about it, he thought, attempting to smile, none whatever: he knew precisely what bitter thing it was, and whence it arose. Slowly and wearily he walked up the path that led to the house.

Four

Is he, Mercy Fellowe breathed at herself in the looking glass, attracted? She often breathed inquiries like this one now. It was clear that he took an interest in her and thought highly of her gifts. Indeed, he was forever quarrying talents in her that she had never suspected. The other day she had drawn, in black chalk on the study wall, a picture of a large angry lady in a ridiculous hat and written below, *Mrs Bentley Burssting Out of the Top Drawer*. When he came in and saw it there he had looked a little surprised, but after examination had told her delightedly that it had all the apparent incoherence and profound underlying lucidity of *The Bride Stripped Bare by Her Bachelors*. She had no idea at all what he meant by this; but there she was, with profound underlying lucidity added onto a remarkable, innate, true eye for an unusual Dufy.

Yes, he was interested: but could he be, she breathed, attracted? The query left a little round of mist on the glass. To me, as a woman? She breathed again, and another little misty globe appeared beside the first. She put out a brown childish finger and drew a nipple on each of them. Slowly the bosom faded away and she was left looking into her own face again. Large green eyes, high cheekbones, snub nose, full lips, all rather Russian. Her mother always said that when she could afford it she must get some of those embroidered peasant blouses that everyone had worn when she, Mrs. Fellowe, had been a "gel," although Mercy hankered privately for tight black satin.

Not beautiful, she now courageously breathed, but amusing?

It was terrible to be so young, terrible not to know what to wear or say or do or what, even secretly, to think. That dragon of a sister, who disliked her so much—why?—always looked so utterly marvellous and she was old. They were twins, yet she was old while he was simply distinguished, mature and sophisticated. How gorgeous, she breathed, to be sophisticated! She placed a hand on her hip and waggled her bottom. But how could anyone be fascinating in a skirt of pleated grey drip-dry terylene? She must lose no time in acquiring the black satin, if she were not to be utterly despised. Her figure was awful, hardly any bosom—a bosom like two tennis balls—such narrow hips, such long legs, such long thin feet. Her ideal of the moment was a Mrs Eva Bernstein who kept a hat shop, and against this ample yardstick she measured herself and found all sadly wanting. But at least, and she thanked God for it, her bottom was shaped like a peach and not like a pear. Sally Goodchild's pear-shaped bottom had cast a shadow over her life.

Could a man desire me? she breathed, and, drooping, decided that for all her underlying lucidity he probably could not. She grew almost faint with despondency. She must eat more and develop a bosom like Eva Bernstein's, she must think of brilliant things to say, she must get mascara for her lashes, she must wrinkle up her forehead and get some lines on it. She would sell her lacrosse stick and buy a length of black satin.

Oh! It was a quarter past ten and she was supposed to be in the study by ten o'clock. She ran downstairs, paused outside the door long enough to get her breath, and entered majestically, swaying a little, with a brown hand pressed to a firm little bosom.

Adorable, Ninian thought. "Late again, my child," he said. "Write to Reynolds and tell him to send photographs of the Bacon pictures to Montevideo. Write to Merrilees and ask him please to send on the two Taplins he is holding to Reynolds."

"Yes, Mr La Touche," she said. How lovely to be ordered about by him, she thought. Or by someone. There was Freddie, she was crazy about the way his hair grew over his ears, but he was not sophisticated. And he lived in a semidetached. There was a sweet confusion in her blood and a delectable disorder in her brain. She wrote to Reynolds and bade him send all the Mary Taplin pictures to Montevideo. I am Ninian's handmaiden, she thought with a voluptuous shiver. Ninian! She had never used his name before, even in her own mind. She looked ardently at his silver hair in between the mistyping of his letters. How I wish he would scold me, laugh at me, trample me underfoot! Was he to be, could he ever, ever be, her first experience?

Five

Two days later, "Love!" said Ninian at breakfast, glancing up from *The Times*, "the world needs love."

The remark was so foreign to his style that Violet, who disliked innovation at any time and in the early morning detested it, looked at him gravely. "I thought you were going to London today," she said, with a satiric eye on his clothes.

"So I was. But I have decided to go sketching instead."

"Sketching!" echoed his sister.

"And pray, Violet, why not? It is time that I cultivated my own talent, high time. I have laboured in the fields of others too long." There was an effervescence about him this morning as of a man embarking on great new things. He finished his kedgeree and took a boiled egg, no portly egg with a pinkish-gold shell such as they were used to but a meagre waxy one with the blurred figure of a lion stamped on it. "Violet, what may this be?"

"That is a shop egg," she explained. "Mrs Bentley wrote to say that an outbreak of poultry disease makes it impossible for her to supply."

"How petty women are!" Ninian smiled.

"And there is to be no more milk and cream," Violet went on. "Mrs Bentley wrote that the long drought has affected the milk and cream."

"We won't be defeated," he told her. He imagined Mrs Bentley's triumphant face, large and crimson as a blown peony, and put the egg back. "Violet, we must get chickens, we must get cows."

"My dear Ninian, but where from? I have no idea where such things are to be got."

"Write to Harrods," he advised her. He had enormous faith in Harrods. Buttering another piece of toast he inquired, "Is there anything more to eat?"

There was more kedgeree or cold Yorkshire ham or Olimpia would grill him kidneys with tomato: she had a way of preparing simple English dishes that displayed them in a new aspect altogether.

"Capital!" he said, rubbing his hands. "Violet, did you hear what I said about love?"

"I did indeed," she answered.

It was odd that he should raise the subject, she thought, at a moment when he was about the most hated man in the locality. Not content with cutting off the supply of eggs and cream, Mrs Bentley made tireless, implacable propaganda against him. An affront to Mrs Bentley, Mrs Bentley in all good faith believed, was little short of an affront to the Almighty, Whom, when she thought of the matter at all, she looked on as the de luxe edition of herself. In the ordinary way people would have paid little attention, for she was not a favourite; but the outrage to Mrs Bentley had to be seen in context with the boorish treatment of Miss Frobisher as that lady studied the *Pythoness, Drinking,* and the truly amazing behaviour to the Women's Institute.

Mrs Harte had written to Ninian saying it might be more convenient if he met the party at the Exhibition itself, rather than travel to London with it: they would be going up on the cheap excursion and Mr La Touche would doubtless prefer his beautiful motor. She had taken it for granted that he would reply saying there were places for three of them in the car with him; but he had not answered at all. It surprised them, for Mr La Touche was so punctilious, it was one of the many things they all liked about him: such a brilliant artistic man and so courteous to humdrum provincials like themselves! But Mary Taplin was having a show, he must be extremely busy. Trustingly they set out on the day itself, but he never appeared. For nearly an hour the little flock had waited in the vestibule of the Academy, reluctant to begin viewing without him lest they admire things they shouldn't and pestering officials to know if a message had come. At last Mrs Rearden put in a call to Silverwood (six-and-nine, but Miss Dugdale kindly said it could be met out of funds) and was answered by Ninian himself, who told her, laughing, that he thought the whole idea must have been a joke!

"The Women's Institute never jokes about culture," Mrs Rearden sternly replied and rang off. They had been, and to a woman still were, furious with him.

"You sound as if you didn't believe in love," Ninian said now, in the same happy way.

"Will you want luncheon, if you are not going up?" was her only reply. She really began to feel like a wife, with all the apologizing and lying. "And what about your secretary?"

"Sandwiches, please. And Mercy has the day off, to go and see her mother in the town," Ninian said, his dark eyes moistening a little. "A most interesting and unusual woman, Violet. Left a widow with no means and a baby daughter, she turned her hand to whatever offered, typing, cooking, sewing. Now she has her own little teashop, just by the Cathedral Close. Funny that I never noticed it. Only think, she makes all her own jams, jellies, cakes and scones!"

"I know the sort of thing," Violet said.

"She calls it 'Close By,' " Ninian said, smiling.

Violet looked at him again and returned to her newspaper. She liked the popular prints, with their court cases and gossip and enthusiasm, and relied on Ninian to inform her on graver matters. "Oh, dear!" she exclaimed presently.

"Well?"

" 'World on point of religious revival . . .' " Violet quavered.

"What did I tell you?" Ninian asked with satisfaction. "Love . . ."

"But Ninian, it's Poppy! Here's a picture of her at the top of a lamppost, with a constable waiting

53

below. 'London's oldest girl about town says world . . .'"

"Violet, please!" Shuddering, he pushed back his chair and hurried out of the room, as he always did when things annoyed him.

All very fine, Violet thought. How pleasant to be a man, and hurry out of rooms! Dismally she reviewed her own situation. Everything to be patched up in the neighbourhood bit by bit, if it were at all possible. Ninian was overworked, ill, mad. Sometime today she must ring up dear Dr Benn. It had come to his ears that Olimpia was treating McCardle for pleurisy—caught, McCardle averred, while planting the deodars—by injections of her own concocting. Mrs Dimble the daily must have spread the news and the doctor's letter this morning implied that he would not visit Silverwood professionally again if the injections continued. Manley wanted to come for the week-end, "provided," he wrote, "that Ninian spares me the tale of secretary and Dufy." How like Manley, to invite himself and make stipulations in the same breath! A room must be got ready, Violet must pick the flowers herself with McCardle laid up, what a nuisance it all was, and there would be the long exhausting struggle to keep the Italians from him. She looked forward, however, to seeing his face when his breakfast eggs had a lion on the shell. Her own face brightened a little at the thought, and fell again as her eye lit on the photograph of Poppy, treed in her lamppost.

Ninian had resolutely driven the thought of Poppy away and now was assembling his gear for work: plump virgin tubes of paint, gleaming palette and glossy brushes, canvas block, brand new stool and easel. Everything was dead right, for he had of course known just what to buy and where to buy it. He hunted out the old straw hat he always wore in Italy, the one that Berenson had given him so many years ago, and clapped it on. To cover his head like that while still indoors made him feel bohemian and somewhat caddish, and he savoured this feeling: he relished too the idea of running off to paint in the fields when Reynolds expected him in London. I am grrrreat arrrrtist! he murmured with a smile, in imitation of Prazhovsky the sculptor, but even as he smiled there was a wild hope, an excitement of his brain, called up by the very words. After all, stranger things had happened. Great talents had found themselves, great work had been done, when the artist was past his youth, look at Gauguin, look at Cervantes.

And look at Granny Moses, his real self intervened.

Ninian ignored this real self, thinking it the only way to deal with that kind of person. He continued to meditate. People imprisoned themselves within a web of fear and sloth and habit and needed only courage and faith to burst through the strands. There was no such thing as being "too old," the idea of age was a conspiracy of others, of the world, and arose from envy. The world would exclaim in censure, "At his time of life!" of someone merely because he did not conform to its notion of what suited, and was not content to be dull and defeated and dead . . .

His preparations concluded, he set forth with the hat still on his head and his hands too full to raise it when he passed Mrs Dimble on the stairs, so that she stood there looking after him, her duster immobile and her mouth open. As he crossed the hall Violet came out of the dining room.

"The sandwiches can come on after me," he said, as if sandwiches were things of reason and movement.

"But where will you be?" she asked, with a look of fear at his hatted head.

"By and by, by and by," he answered cheerily, his mind full of art and love and age and hope.

He intended to paint the wheat field this side of Mary Taplin's house: the gold stalks of the wheat stubble, the purple tones of the shadow between the sheaves, the dark mill behind and the stretch of tree-fringed river, these he had noted on his last visit to her. He had thought them a beautiful subject for someone to paint and, in that same moment, had realized that he wanted to be a painter himself and would become one. Without wasting a day he had written off for the paints and canvases and the rest of his equipment.

He walked on, feeling as if he were twenty once more. Everything this morning appeared to him as delightful or touching or funny. Autumn was at its peak, fiery hedges, dazzling bushes, trees ablaze, the bracken a pale gold, fat berries dawdling on the bough, all resplendent in the sun, all smiling and making the most of themselves as if aware that it could not last much longer. There was a delicious nip of frost in the air. Farmer Warren's bull was racing the little blue local train known as The Duffer. This animal loved above all things to match his speed against that of others. Strangers walking through his field would hear the thunder of his hooves and flee in terror, they would hear him gradually closing on them, abandoning all hope at last they would piteously recommend their souls to heaven. Then the bull would lightly gallop past and, having made his point, turn off in a half circle and make for something else. Ninian was overjoyed to see him gaining steadily on The Duffer, concerning which the local newspaper was always full of complaints. A monster screamed through the air just then and broke the barrier just overhead; both bull and train, hearing this, put on a little burst of speed.

It was not only in response to things about him that he felt young. He was conscious of a myriad possibilities within, as untried youth often is. Painting had been decided on, but he could equally well have written, navigated, composed, invented or laid down a system of philosophy: all manner of gifts and powers and energies seemed to be tumbling about in his mind like the waves of a troubled sea.

He came to the wheat field and set up easel and stool. As he squeezed paint on to the new palette he smiled at his own impatience. The whole thing was arranged and ready in his brain, a completed picture waiting only to be transferred to the canvas. He had long ago acquired the painter's habit of seeing mass, form, movement, light, shade where others saw trees, sky, houses, men and women. The act of painting itself, well-nigh miraculous to the uninitiated, was but a simple mechanical affair beside this power of seeing and composing. He reached out with a brush, hesitated, reached out again, then put the brush in his left hand and mixed some more colour. He repeated this cycle a few times more; and then looked at the scene with half-closed eyes and pursed lips. Come now, he thought. It was getting silly. He knew exactly how to begin, by setting down an object like a small peppermill in sepia, to the right of and above the centre of the canvas. That was Mary Taplin's house and when it was in, and the trees along the river and the five-barred gate at the left far corner of the wheat field, he would have his skeleton.

Solemn, cautious, like a man about to throw a dart, he advanced his brush again. Then he took it back and sat for a few moments, wriggling his toes in irritation. Surely, he reasoned, anyone can paint an object like a small peppermill in sepia? But what size peppermill, in all this great arch of blue and gold and purple? With a severe, important look on his face he sat making fussy little movements with his brush as clerks do with their pens when unable to collect their thoughts. The chief thing was to make a start of a kind, of any kind at all, and build on from there.

No more nonsense, come, he said to himself.

He plunged recklessly at the canvas, painting at random with fierce rapid strokes, and drew his head back to consider the result. The figure on the canvas did not in any way suggest Mary's house or a peppermill but it had, he told himself, an arresting quality of its own. Gaunt, extenuated, ominous, it might have been a toadstool painted by El Greco. I am undoubtedly an Expressionist, he thought with satisfaction, as he began to mix the paint for the trees.

Something happened then which drove all else from his head. It was as if a great iron hand gripped him by the chest and was closing on it ever more tightly and cruelly, until his heart and lungs could hardly work and the pain ran down his arms to the tips of his fingers. He shut his eyes, dizzy, white-faced. "Violet, please come to me," he whispered, gentle and humble as a little boy. Then slowly the grip began to loosen again, until he was free of it and sat gasping, with tears in his eyes.

He had no illusions: it was death. A curious awareness of the approach of death had been, he saw in a flash, the real cause of the alternating joy, despair and frenzy of all this latter time. The desire to paint had been a last welling up of love for a beautiful world from which he must separate and a last impulse to leave something of himself behind in it. That sudden revelation to him, as he read *The Times* at breakfast, of the world's need for more and ever more love had been an intimation that this day, or one day very soon, would be his last. How clear it all was now! and he had been thinking of fresh life, renewed youth, unrealized powers, and even . . . No fool like an old fool, his real self gibed, insufferable even in a moment like this.

Now the hand gripped him again, so terribly that a kind of animal sobbing burst from his lips. "Oh, Violet, won't you come?" he pleaded. "Do come, Violet." The hideous pain flowed everywhere, into his neck, his hands, the calves of his legs. His eyes were open and staring but he saw nothing, yet was aware of such trivial matters as the cold sweat on his back with his shirt clinging to it, and that a bee hummed tediously near by. Violet, you *must* come! But now the grip was relaxing. Evidently he was not to go quite yet.

For an hour and more he waited but the pain did not come again. There was no fear or rebellion or anguish in his heart but only a tranquil and compassionate love for all created beings. He thought kindly now even of Poppy, whom he saw as struggling in a trap with the rest of humanity. Such was the serenity of his mind at this moment that he could look on all the beauty of the country lying before him without envy or grief.

Presently he made up his mind to try and walk as far as Mary's house. She would send for the doctor, who would arrange for him to enter a nursing home if anything were still to be gained by it and who in any case would break the news gently to Violet. Tears came to Ninian's eyes as he thought of Violet at home, unconscious of the blow about to fall, at that very moment perhaps writing to Harrods about the cows and chickens that now would never be wanted. Gingerly and with frequent pauses for rest he made his way through the rasping stalks of wheat, opened the gate at the far end with infinite care, and crept to the Taplins' door.

Oliver Knox opened the door and frowned. "She's painting," he said with his most ungracious manner.

"I am sorry indeed to intrude upon you," Ninian replied with gentle forgiveness. "I have just had two severe heart attacks and find myself unable to reach home. Will you allow me to telephone to Benn?"

On hearing himself thus appealed to, on being treated as—in the curious phrase he favoured—a person in his own right, Oliver's demeanour changed entirely and he begged the sufferer to come in and rest while he himself saw to the telephoning. He helped him to a sofa, put cushions behind his head as gently as any woman, fetched water and brandy and hurried away to ring up the doctor. Soon he bustled in again with a rug for Ninian's poor feet.

"He's coming at once. He was just about to leave for hospital, but," Oliver said with deep satisfaction, "I told him it was a matter of life and death."

"You are very good," Ninian murmured, closing his eyes and leaning back so as to be in character.

"Oh, not at all. We mustn't let you slip through our fingers before Mary's show comes on."

Ninian smiled weakly.

"Well, well, well, La Touche, so we're in the wars again," Dr Benn said cheerfully, running into the room and opening his bag like a man with no time to lose. "What's our trouble today? Taplin says it's a heart attack. Nonsense!"

Ninian described his experience in the wheat field simply but vividly and, with the air of one who lives only for others, entreated the doctor to take on himself the task of breaking the news to Violet.

"We don't know what news to break so far," Dr Benn replied with a twinkle. "Open the shirt, please."

"My days are numbered, Benn," Ninian told him quietly and bravely. "Odd, how we always know."

"Say Ah, will you? Again. Again. I wish I had a fiver," the doctor chuckled, "for every deathbed of yours that I have attended over the years. Hold still, would you?" He listened and tapped, listened and tapped, while the amusement gradually died out of his cherubic face. When the examination was over he folded his hands and looked at Ninian with something akin to horror.

"There you are!" the moribund said, not without a touch of complacence.

"La Touche," said the doctor solemnly, "a physician must always hear the whole story, however horrible or shameful it may be. Tell me the truth, like a man. What did you have for breakfast this morning?" He was as kindly, humane and reasonable as man could be save in respect of food, which he would have liked to abolish altogether; and as the patient made his halting admissions violent irrepressible shudders ran up and down his little frame. "Ham! Kidneys! *Kedgeree!*" he screamed. "You disgust me, La Touche. You fill me with loathing. I am done with you forever."

He clapped everything into the bag with hands that shook and dashed from the room. In a moment or two he dashed in again.

"Boa constrictor!" he said, but quietly and sadly now, the friend rather than the man of science.

"I suddenly felt so well and young," Ninian said in a low, troubled voice.

"You are not young," the doctor replied, "and now thanks to this repulsive orgy you are not even well. Gorging yourself in a way that even a growing boy, a growing boy . . . what am I saying?" he panted, ". . . that a growing ostrich would think twice about." He rushed out of the room and in again. "A woman of your age walked across America, eating mainly grass," he said. "Do you imagine you could walk across America, eating mainly grass?"

"I shouldn't dream of walking across America at all," the patient replied with a flicker of spirit.

"Sneer if you like," the doctor retorted. "I am going. You have made me late at the hospital, where there are people who really need me."

"Really, Benn, I do assure you, it was agony. I have never been in such pain before. Why," argued Ninian, "instead of fulminating in this very unprofessional manner do you not at least tell me what the matter was?"

"Wind," said the doctor cuttingly. "And if you want my professional advice, you will fast for twenty-four hours and never do it again. But I will run you home, after all. You have made me so late that a few minutes more will hardly signify and there is something I wish to say to Miss La Touche."

"Not anything very serious, I hope?" Oliver Knox said anxiously as the two men were leaving. He began to wonder what Mary would say when she heard of the episode. "Shall I call my wife? I'm sure that if you are ill . . ."

"No, no," Ninian said sheepishly. "Benn is going to take me home. I . . . at my time of life . . . must expect . . . have to go quietly. . . ."

Dr Benn loudly blew his nose.

"Well, goodbye, and thank you for everything, Taplin." Ninian hurried away with Oliver looking after him, his cheeks drawn and pinched as if he were sucking a lemon.

The doctor was too fond of human beings in general and of Ninian in particular to remain angry for long, even when faced with so vile an example of depravity as his; and by the time he drew up at Silverwood he was quite himself again. Violet was just about to leave the house with Ninian's sandwiches and looked inquiringly at them as they came in together.

"I've brought Master Billy Bunter home," Dr

Benn said gaily. "I found him on show in a circus, the centre of an animated throng. My dear Miss La Touche"—and now he became serious and gentle in manner and spoke as if they were alone together—"I was going to ring you up. Do ignore my stupid letter. Throw it away. Restrain the enterprising Olimpia if you can, but do not fear, or hope, that my visits here will cease."

"I never did," Violet answered. Her colour rose slightly, making her look younger and less forbidding. Ninian was pleased by what he took for concern on his behalf, although he never quite approved of the bantering tone his sister used when speaking of him to the doctor. "I'm sorry about Olimpia but I doubt if I can restrain her. I cannot even restrain my brother."

"Very likely not. Overeating is a sign of emotional disturbance," Dr Benn said. "He may be one of those crazy mixed-up kids they make the films about."

"Enough," Ninian put in. "You forget all I've been through."

"What have you been through?" Violet said, pricking up her ears. "Nothing very much, I fancy, or I should have known of it somehow. Is that, may I ask, your morning's work?" She looked appraisingly at the brown blot on the canvas. "I expected it to be bad, but not quite as meagre."

"Rome wasn't built in a day," her brother replied, flourishing a hand in the air to emphasize his entire self-confidence. "When next you see that masterpiece it may well contain a five-barred gate."

"And where are your paints?"

"I left them in the field," he said lamely.

"Did you know that we had a genius in the family?" Violet asked Dr Benn.

The doctor examined the daub and reproachfully shook his head. "Give me photographs," he said. "There's no fooling with photographs."

"Oh! Reynolds telephoned," Violet said to Ninian. "He sounded very vexed but the line was bad and I didn't hear it all. Something about Montevideo and are you mad. If," she wearily observed, "I have been asked that once lately I have been asked it twenty times."

"He's an old fussbox," Ninian said. "Come now, Benn, don't you detect a Spanish feeling in that house?"

"House? I thought it was a cactus. No, no, La Touche," the doctor said decidedly, "give me a camera every time. I like to know where I am."

Violet took off her hat and put her basket down. "And so I cut sandwiches for nothing," she said. "What would you like for luncheon, Ninian?"

"Nothing at all," Dr Benn said firmly. "Everyone eats too much. My breakfast consists of a glass of water. At our time of life there is little need of food or none. Little or none."

Six

"My dear Manley! How nice to see you."

"You didn't mind my asking myself?"

As Manley invariably did this the La Touches were surprised by the question.

"But of course not," Ninian said. "Please do, whenever you want to come."

In descending on Silverwood at this time Manley had two objects in view apart from a constant third, which was to live as much as possible at the expense of others. Rumours concerning La Touche and his secretary were beginning to fly in Oxford and London, and he wished to inform himself as to the facts. The keenest and cruellest gossip alive, he scrutinized the secrets of his friends with the same patience and care that he brought to historical research, never repeating without verification and verifying where he could at source: nor did he feel it as a restriction since, nine times in ten, the truth was more delightfully and wildly absurd than any fable.

His second, more pressing object was to make headway in the matter of the Italian pair, who after all this time seemed as firmly rooted as ever. Early in the coming year the first volume of Manley's magnum opus on the Portuguese overseas empire would be published by the Oxford and Yale University Presses simultaneously. He had vowed that by then, were it humanly possible, Olimpia should be cooking for him alone. He loved to envisage himself as wholly triumphant, basking in the warmth of public glory and private bliss. But how could he get her to himself for long enough to plead his cause in the beautiful Italian and dazzle her with the tales of the villa near Battipaglia? One or other of the La Touches was forever at his side: one would have thought, he told himself indignantly, that they did not trust him. The dinner Olimpia sent up on his first evening filled him with sadness, almost with despair. He was like a man with a vision of beauty before his eyes that he feels may never be grasped and enjoyed. Now and again in the course of that noble meal he shut his eyes as music lovers do at a concert, and when he laid his fork down for the last time the others saw that those same little eyes were bright with unshed tears.

"We nearly didn't have your show," Ninian said to Mary, as the men came into the drawing room later on. "Mercy tried to send all the pictures to Montevideo." He was smiling proudly.

"What made her change her mind?" Mary asked.

"She was foiled by stuffy old Reynolds. But, we may depend on it, she will think of something new very shortly. She has the most original mind of anyone I know."

"Thank you," Manley said.

"She also has a natural true eye," Ninian blithely swept on. He related the affair of the Dufy, while the historian looked down his short nose.

"How very nice for her," Mary said vaguely. Like many people of creative power she was not impressed by expertise.

"You sound as if you didn't believe me," Ninian said with reproach. "She is such a many-sided, gifted girl. She has done a charcoal drawing on my study wall that Duchamp himself could hardly have improved on."

"So we may thank Miss Fellowe for that horrid mess," Violet said.

"Violet!" Ninian looked as amazed and hurt as if she had slapped him. "How can you speak so? You have always been against her, you have never given her a chance," he said passionately, speaking as if the two of them were alone in the room. "It has been like that from the beginning. I have hardly known you in these last weeks. Mary, my dear," he said, turning to her and using a tone of appeal, "please come and see the drawing. Violet will pay some attention to you, perhaps."

"Oliver says I am to be home by ten o'clock," Mary began in alarm. She shrank from the idea of arbitrating, her habit being always to agree with everyone impartially. People often discussed this way of hers, some thinking it came of weakness, others that she was too kind to contradict: the truth was she very seldom listened to what was said at all. "He so dislikes our being separated for any length of time."

"Then he should have come too, as he was invited to do," Violet said.

"Ninian called him 'Taplin,' " Mary explained.

"Dear, dear! And so you will obediently trot home in the middle of the evening?"

"I would do anything," Mary said gravely.

"For Oliver?" Violet smiled, to take the sting from what she was saying.

"For peace."

Violet looked at her with new interest.

Ninian declared that it would not take more than a moment and, deaf to Mary's entreaties, bore her away. He was thoroughly roused and determined to see justice done. Violet's attitude to the young, brilliant, helpless girl that destiny, or chance, or whatever you liked to call it, had brought to their door was ignoble, no other word would do, and could only result from some mean feminine jealousy of her youth and gifts and mysterious fascination.

"Please wait a moment," he said at the study door. "I want to arrange the lighting perfectly before you see it."

"Come on!" he called presently.

Mary came to a halt in front of the drawing and looked unhappy.

"Well?" he said, unable to keep the irritation out of his voice.

"My dear Ninian!" she murmured. So it's true, she thought.

"Is that all you have to say?" he cried.

"Ninian, I can't pretend about these things." Mary looked round helplessly like a tormented animal seeking a way of escape.

"You are entitled to have an opinion," he said coldly. "Artists are known to be not the best judges of other artists."

"That is true," she assented eagerly.

"I may not have your talent, but you will concede that I have just a little, a *very* little, judgment?" he went on. "It was I, you may remember, who discovered Isolowolotumba, Prazhovsky, Gazpacho and Dodds. Everyone laughed me to scorn."

"Quite so," she said humbly.

"Then, my dear Mary"—and he laid a forgiving arm round her shoulder—"do you not think it possible that you may be wrong?"

"No."

"How can you be so . . . so *feminine*," he exclaimed.

Mary smiled at him, thinking he really sounded very much like Oliver at times. Probably, she reflected, all men were very much like Oliver when you got to know them. Her smile died away, but not before it had irritated Ninian further.

"In one breath you agree that you may be a poor judge, in the next you say you cannot be mistaken," he scolded.

"Yes, because there is nothing to be mistaken about," she replied. "If there was, I might well be. But perhaps," she said, at her wit's end, "she is musical or something?"

"Tchah!" Ninian looked upwards and raised both

arms, as if appealing to the Creator he did not believe in. Then he replaced the table lamp which he had put on its side to floodlight the mural and turned it off with a sharp click. Opening the door for her he said in a tone so gentle and kind as to be offensive, "Let us go down." They walked along the passage to the stairs without a word, to come on Violet hurrying up to them with an air of agitation.

"Manley has seen a monkey," she said. "I asked him to pull the curtains for me, and it looked through the window at him."

"Probably his own reflection," Ninian said, declining to take any interest.

"I naturally thought of that," she replied, "but he described it to me, skipping about in the shrubs. A very small one, with long greenish hair and sad eyes."

Her brother shrugged his shoulders.

"I wondered if it was something to do with Miss Fellowe," Violet said.

Ninian stopped dead, his face white. "Violet," he said, "if you cannot refrain from slandering that child I shall leave the house."

"I meant nothing," Violet said with tears in her voice. "Mary, was there any harm in what I said? Why else should a monkey be here? Miss Fellowe has initiated so much since she came."

He walked on without replying.

"I say, though," Mary put in, "did Manley invent it? Did he want you out of the way, so that he could work on Olimpia?"

"Mary, you're a genius!" Ninian exclaimed, turning round again. "And we are playing into his hands. Come!"

71

Their differences forgotten for a time, they swept down the stairs together, purposeful and aggressive. The La Touches had always known that one day or another this matter would come to a head. Both were quite convinced that Mary was right; and Violet blamed herself severely for having fallen into the trap. Their attitude was common to the historian's entire range of acquaintance. A charge, no matter how disgraceful, had only to be brought against him for all present to feel in their bones that it must be true. No one who knew him had ever been known to say, "Manley wouldn't do a thing like that."

In the drawing room they found one of the windows thrown up and Manley leaning out into the darkness. "There he goes!" came in a muffled voice. A sharp moist wind blew inwards and made them all shiver.

"Do come in and shut the window," Violet said, "otherwise we shall catch our deaths."

"It is hopping about, just outside," Manley reported.

"I expect it is a witch," Mary said. "Tonight is Halloween."

"Good Lord, already? It can't be." Ninian sounded thoroughly vexed, as if time had no right to pass except under his supervision.

"You are not very interested in the monkey," Manley complained.

"Oh yes we are," Violet told him, "it is just that we don't want to get pneumonia."

At this Manley drew his head in, slammed the window down and turned to face them. "You don't believe there is a monkey, do you?" he said furiously.

"Yes, yes, yes, we do," Ninian replied, thinking how much like one Manley himself looked. "What do you say to a game of chess, Manley? I must have my revenge for last time."

"You don't believe there is a monkey," the other repeated, and now the fury had dropped and a note of pathos was creeping in. "Ninian, I swear to you by all . . ."

"No need, no need," Ninian broke in hastily, as if determined to save an old friend from perjuring himself. "If you tell us there is a monkey we naturally believe you. But, my dear fellow, what of it? Life must go on. Are the ladies to be annoyed and incommoded merely because a monkey chooses to settle in our shrubbery?" he continued lightly and gaily, going to the window to draw the curtain again. Two little eyes with infinite sadness in their depths peered through the glass into his. "Violet!" he exclaimed. "There's a monkey here! Just think of it! There's a monkey here! Just think of it! There's a monkey outside the window, sitting on a branch of the prunus!"

"What did I say?" Manley asked in a tragic voice, folding his arms.

The little creature now hopped on the window sill and tapped in a peremptory fashion on the pane with its knuckles, looking into the room with close-set eyes. When Ninian opened to it and called, however, it darted from the branch to the ground and clumsily scampered away on all fours. "I'll hunt it," Ninian said excitedly, "and Violet, you stay here," for he was still inclined to believe the monkey was part of a ruse. Manley commenced to mutter something about an apology. Ninian scrambled through the window without heeding either him or Mary, who again was attempting to take her leave. Pulling the window down behind him he groped his way through the leaves and twigs while the tiny figure skipped on ahead, turning round now and again as if they were out together by mutual agreement and coughing and sneezing theatrically as if to make fun of the English climate. It was the full of the moon, the hunter's; and the idea of chasing a monkey through the peaceful dignified old garden by its light captivated Ninian entirely. Why had he fired up at poor Violet? He now saw that this was, and could only be, Mercy's handiwork. He would like to see Manley think of anything half as good! Well named, he thought, the heaven-sent Mercy to a man dying of thirst. She was the lunatic goddess of Silverwood, the enchantress, the liberatrice: she it was who, driving away the Bentleys and Reardens, scattering the forces of ennui like a tidal wave washing away the dusty accretions of community life, planted strange happy forests in their midst and beckoned to exotic beasts to come and inhabit them. It was as if a painting of Le Douanier Rousseau had become animated on this moonlit October night and he, Ninian La Touche, were somehow living in it.

While his thoughts ran in this way the monkey, chattering and scolding, led him through the sleeping rose gardens by the sundial into a patch of chrysanthemums that were McCardle's pride and joy, intended by him for the autumn show. Evidently the little creature had passed this way before, as a dozen or so huge snowy blooms lay about on the ground like so many sliced-off curly heads. So terrible a sight would once have made Ninian's blood run cold: now in his antic madness he laughed aloud for very glee.

A tall stooping figure in evening dress came round the wall as he stood there laughing and said apprehensively: "Ni-Ni-Ni . . . inian? I say, I'm fuf-fuf-fuf fearfully sorry."

"Billy!" The spell was broken and all the pleasure gone. What had seemed like a fairy extravaganza now proved to be nothing but some more of Billy Box's nonsense. "I might have known it!"

Billy's brother Alfred was a distinguished physiologist who, to Billy's great distress, conducted experiments on living animals. He and others had explained to Billy time and again that no unnecessary suffering was caused them, that Science must advance and Humanity come first; but while Billy agreed in principle, in practice he could not bear it, and he had only to find out that some little being had passed into the cages of Sir Alfred's laboratory to effect, with remarkable cunning persistence and bravado, its escape.

"Wow-wow-wow would you like it?" he used to say.

"Look at those chrysanthemums," Ninian went on sternly. "McCardle's heart will break."

Unhappily for the La Touches, Sir Alfred's organization was at Oxford, which meant only an hour's drive to the southwest to Silverwood, where Billy considered the environment just the thing for refugee animals and where the physiologist would never dream, or never so far had dreamed, of looking for them. Rats, guinea pigs, hamsters, mice, dogs, all had come its way, and one April there had been a veritable plague of frogs; but this was the first monkey.

75

"I'll bub-bub-bub . . . uy him some more," the conductor promised in remorse.

"He was going to exhibit them," Ninian cried passionately. "Poor good decent old McCardle!"

"So he c-c-can," said the detrimental Box. "Who's gug-gug-gug going to be a pup-pup-pup penny the wiser?"

The monkey was capering from one fruit tree to the next, tearing off the last apples, pears or medlars that hung from the branches, mumbling each for an instant before furiously tossing it away, and doing untold damage to young twigs and shoots.

"And now what? Where is your car?" Ninian used the patient, controlled voice of people addressing madmen.

Billy explained that his car was halfway up the drive, the point where the monkey had suddenly leaped out of it. "But we must catch the mum-mum-mum monkey first," he insisted. "Otherwise she will d-d-die."

"That might help you to realize, Billy, that to do good in this world is not as easy as you think." Ninian spoke simply and impressively and as a father might. Clichés began to roll from his lips in pompous succession: he asked Billy if he thought his brother a less kindly or humane man than himself, and if he, Billy, would prefer the monkey's life to a child's, say his own child's if he had one, and did he realize the marvellous medical discoveries that had resulted from the work of such men as Sir Alfred, discoveries that helped clear away the load of terror and misery from human life; and, finally, if everyone behaved like Billy where would we all be?

"Wow-wow-wow would you like it?" Billy replied.

"Oh, curse you, Billy!"

The monkey now had perched on a wall and, motionless, looked superciliously down on them like a tiny gargoyle. The whole affair struck Ninian as utterly ludicrous and infuriating, not even to think of the day of reckoning when McCardle should rise from his bed. A kind of frenzy came over him. He felt that he, a man wishing only to lead his life, of which so much had been wasted, so much had passed without his heeding it, was surrounded by idiots and bores, in particular Violet with her dull everyday face, who dragged him mercilessly down to trivial concerns of their own or involved him in childish pranks. He wanted to go away and dream of Mercy, and count the minutes until she returned from the week end with her mother. Instead, he must hang about in the cold night air and consider ways and means of capturing a monkey (who had never been asked to come). A twinge in the lumbar region helped to exacerbate his feelings of anger and frustration.

"You've given me lumbago, between you," he added.

Now the spruce little figure of Tito came tripping towards them through the moonlight, fresh, alert and gay as at every moment of day or night. "Signori!" he hailed them, "la Signora send-a me collect-a la scimmia." And he laughed delightedly, as if at a capital joke.

"It will be easier said than done," Ninian said grimly.

The little man clasped his hands and fell back a step in admiration of the heraldic figure on the wall.

"Che bella, ma che bella!" he exclaimed. "Che sara per l'Olimpia una gioia stupenda, inordinata! Sempre, sempre desiderava una come questa!" Gently he approached the wall, clucking, hissing, warbling, cooing by turns, his arms stretched out: gingerly the little animal stepped from her perch into them and laid her cheek on his: together they proceeded to the house, two hearts idyllically beating as one.

"Italy!" murmured Box.

"Yes, Italy is rather special," Ninian agreed. With the sudden happy ending of the difficulty his mood had changed again in the mercurial way it had nowadays. The ease and grace and warmth of his servant moved him, and the little scene enacted with such perfect simplicity before them he had found delightful. "Everyone thinks Italians are cruel to animals," he said with a laugh.

Billy laughed as well. "Have you nun-nun-nun noticed that what everyone thinks is always wr-wr-wrong?" he said.

The doctrine admirably suited La Touche in his present frame of mind. "Come up to the house," he said. "You will have to stay the week end with us. I won't hear of anything else. The only snag is, Manley is here. But together we may be a match for him."

Mirth began to bubble again in his soul. It greatly increased when they got to the drawing room and found the extraordinary scene in progress there.

Left at home by himself, Oliver Knox had adhered to the routine of behaviour that he followed at such times. All through the supper that Mary had cooked and left ready he had fumed and fretted, holding an imaginary diatribe against her for not refusing the invitation to Silverwood as he had done. What sort of wife, he had asked her more than once, associated with people who slighted her husband? It was not that he had anything against the name of Taplin, he told her kindly and reasonably. It was true that he was descended from Scottish kings, but the bourgeois descendants of Huguenot merchants could not be expected to know that. Still less did he deny that to some extent she had "made a name" for herself. That was not to say that her husband should take that name and become a mere appanage of hers. She would do well to remember that he was not a complete nobody. Indeed had he so wished, he said, looking frankly and firmly into where her eyes would have been were she present, he might have made just a little more noise in the world than she had done. He happened to feel out of sympathy with the age, and thus preferred to remain silent.

Having run through this rubric for the thousandth time, he fell a prey to a fear that was the more terrible for being imprecise. He might lose her, she might not come back at all, she might even then be plotting with the La Touches how best to leave him, or might stay so long with them that they suspected that her home life was unhappy. He determined to go and fetch her away, as a husband had every right to do; and, first drinking a quarter-bottle of brandy to give him heart, set out in fighting trim. It was some little distance to go, Mary having taken the car, and his mood had gradually shifted along the way until he had arrived at Silverwood in a condition of pure benevolence, persuaded that on this night he was destined to win all hearts. For the past twenty minutes and more he had been holding unshakeably forth while Violet and Manley stared at him in indignation and Mary thought of something else.

"You take some honey," he was saying, with his mouth slewed a little to one side in the effort of concentration. He was expounding to them his personal method of trapping flies. Stabbing his left palm with his right forefinger he went on: "Now, slit up a paper bag. Take your honey and *smear it evenly over the paper,* taking good care not to get it over your clothes . . ."

"Ninian!" cried Violet in a strangled voice. "Did Tito catch the monkey?"

"He did indeed," her brother said, smiling, "and I caught Billy, so there's been a rich haul altogether."

"You then extend the paper in a situation where you have reason to believe flies will assemble in quantity," Oliver proceeded loudly. "There is no need for you to stay after that: the trap acts on its own."

"You're going to stay the night?" Violet said. "If everyone will excuse me, I'll see to Billy's room." She hurried out.

"The beauty of this system is efficiency first, and also cheapness," Oliver shouted.

"It sounds nothing if not practicable, Taplin," Ninian said heartily. He thought the man deserved encouragement for silencing Manley in that accomplished way.

Oliver jumped up and said "Come along, do" to Mary, who by now had given up hope of ever prising him from his chair. "Good night, Stanley," he said to Manley, who ignored him altogether.

"I'm so very glad you were not ill," Mary said, holding Ninian's hand for a moment.

"Thank you, my dear," he said, understanding and forgiving. "And your great day will be on us at any moment. I'll be there all the time—no effort shall be spared for the finest woman painter I know, even if she does not appreciate her fellow artist M.F."

"Come on, girl, come on," Oliver said harshly, making for the door.

"But I feel quite sure she is musical," Mary said, as she prepared to follow. "She has such a pretty voice."

"Or literary?" Manley suggested. "Could we, perhaps, find her a little reviewing for the T.L.S.?"

Ninian thoughtfully considered the point. "I'm not sure if she is quite ready for that," he said then, and accompanied the Knoxes to their motor car. A strange pair, he thought as they drove away, even physically ill assorted, Mary large and warm with her yellow hair and peachy skin and Oliver small and dark and pigeon-chested. Why had she done it? What had she seen? But there was no rhyme or reason in such things: they simply happened, he told himself. The rest of the world could only look on in mystification.

Seven

"I seem to have taken rather a lot of cream," Manley remarked at breakfast next morning, with a touch of defiance.

In fact he had taken it all: his ample helping of stewed fruit lay buried under the entire contents of the jug. He felt no remorse for this act, being in a peculiarly disagreeable frame of mind. The affair of the monkey still rankled, for deliberate falsehood was a thing—it might be said the one thing—of which he could not be accused. Both Violet and Ninian must have known this well and yet by their demeanour had suggested that the monkey was a fiction, thus denying to him the only virtue he had. Then as he came into the breakfast room this morning eagerly expecting to see the usual array of silver dishes there, their lids to be raised one after the other with his pudgy hand, their various inviting fragrances to be snuffed at with his button of a nose, he saw only a collection of boiled eggs: eggs, moreover, that were small and greyish with a lion inked on their shells. He took it as a hint that his presence at Silverwood was unwelcome; but since no mere hint would ever have removed him and since this too was surely known to the La Touches, the whole thing struck him as an idle gesture of hostility.

"And the village dairy is shut on Sundays," Violet said, as if one jugful of cream were all she kept in the house.

"The village dairy?" echoed Manley, with the air of a late Roman emperor apprised of yet another barbarian advance. "Pray, Violet, what can you mean?"

"Mrs Bentley refuses to supply us," Ninian said. He spoke indulgently, as if Mrs Bentley's decision were some little feminine caprice.

"But Mrs Bentley is not the only pebble on the beach," expostulated the irate historian. "What about Lord Symington? Have you tried Lord Symington? You must try Lord Symington."

This was a Labour peer and local grandee who had begun life as a hotel page, worked and schemed his way through various unions to national eminence and now kept one of the finest dairy herds in the country.

"We feel it would be trading with the enemy," Ninian said.

"Is this the explanation of those nasty objects over there?" Manley demanded, pointing at the eggs on the sideboard.

"I fear so," Violet said, "although they are not as nasty as they look. Strange that it should be so: people are often still nastier," she concluded, on a note of reverie.

"Does the Bentley woman not know that you entertain?" Manley went on querulously. "I never could like her. Buck House and dukes to lunch and that dire shire sense of humour!" Billy looked up from his egg and said, "You mum-mum-mum . . . ustn't say things like that on Suh-Suh-Suh Sunday."

"Am I to contain myself for twenty-four hours in deference to your opinion? Violet," he addressed her in tones of immense self-pity, "you might *at least,* knowing how fond I am of them, have put on a few devilled bones."

"Olimpia has to have a rest now and then," Violet returned, unmoved.

She was herself unaware of the reason for the vacancies in the breakfast board and feared that the jewel was indisposed. So excellent were the Riccis both in their separate spheres that instructions hardly had to be given. Olimpia had been told long ago that Mr Manley craved her devilled bones and until now had seen to it that he always got them. But the truth of it was, she had so taken to the monkey from the first moment of their introduction that she could think of nothing else. It was Tito who had boiled the eggs and made the coffee, chocolate, tea and toast. His wife had stayed up till all hours, making the little creature a bed, a jacket, some lemon and honey for her poor throat, a comforter for her wheezy chest: she had sung much of *La Traviata* to her and given several injections; and when at last the lovingly impatient Tito had commanded her to bed she had, in his very embrace, thoroughly put him off his stroke by demanding if the name "Desdemona," that of a small sister now sleeping in the arms of Jesus, but for all that sadly missed on earth to this day, would not be a charming and appropriate one for the newcomer.

Having finished his fruit Manley approached the eggs, chose the biggest with enviable directness, returned to his place and peevishly sliced off the top, to discover beneath it a yellow waxy substance with lavender marbling.

"Oh, I say, look here!" he exclaimed to the table at large. Then as the smell reached his nostrils he clapped a hand to his nose, jumped to his feet and ran away.

Such a thing as a bad egg had never been known at Silverwood before. For a few seconds brother and sister were paralysed with consternation. Ninian was the first to recover, the shame of it touching him not so closely, and with great firmness and presence of mind rang for Tito: who, on entering and sizing things up, removed the egg with Latin phlegm to the kitchen, where he and Olimpia all but died of laughing and Desdomona shrieked and clapped her tiny wrinkled palms.

It was a poor beginning to Sunday; and that Manley should have been the victim was particularly to be deplored. Long ago the La Touches had agreed, or rather Ninian had decided and Violet had acquiesced, that the historian was to have all the toleration that lay within the power of their frail human natures. Two things contributed to this decision: Ninian's respect for intellectual achievement and his compassion for one whom he looked on as a monster. Short of refusing to see him at all, there was nothing else for it. Old Mrs Manley had told Ninian before she died that she had been greatly helped by regarding her son as a cross, and had been able to feel, in his presence, that in spirit and in truth she followed her Lord to Calvary; but Ninian had no mystical consolation of this kind. Only, when stung by some new atrocity to loathing, he would take down a volume of Manley's work and read over some pages of his prose, finding there the strength to persevere a while longer.

"Violet, what shall we do?" he murmured now.

"I'll go and speak to him," she said, equally subdued.

"Lul-lul leave him alone and he may gug-gug-gug go away," Billy advised. Manley roused in his gentle heart feelings that otherwise he kept for his brother and the Musicians' Union.

Violet shook a finger at him and left the room. Ninian suddenly and almost without meaning to broke into a laugh. In the shock of realizing that Manley's egg was bad, the dismay of seeing a guest, no matter whom, abruptly leave his table, he had responded traditionally and as a host would. Now the demon was back, to whisper how charming disorder, even outrage, was, how delightful the slackening of bonds, the breaking away, the departures. His regret now was that the episode had not been pre-arranged.

He was half inclined to overtake Violet in pursuit of the fugitive Manley and blurt out to that umbrageous character something that should make an awkward situation irreparable. Henceforth, he felt, there must above all else be novelty: new forms of life, of thought, of behaviour. He told himself that he had lived under restraint for too long.

"You'll be going in to your Matins, I daresay?" he said now. "I'll come with you, if I may."

"Of course," Billy agreed, staring. Ninian's rarely heard laugh startled him, and the request he made even more. Billy's simple religious devotion had long been a joke of the La Touches, and as a rule he set out for church from their house amid an ironic banter in which affection mingled with a slight contempt. Half an hour later he was yet more surprised when Ninian came downstairs, ready to leave. He had changed into a suit of tweed assembling the wildest colours known to the peasantry of Donegal, although it was woven, for otherwise he would never have come across it, by an exclusive house in Milan; and in the hall he put over this a new overcoat with wide, squared shoulders and a tie belt. On his head a black beret already perched at a rakish angle; and this, and the fact that he held neither gloves nor prayer book, caused the musician to look at him attentively.

"Are you c-c-coming to the Cathedral like that?" he asked.

"My dear Billy, I'm not coming in!" Ninian exclaimed. "I have business near by, that's all. Close by!" He sighed with pleasure and folded his hands in his lap.

"Good! I mum-mum must say, you look rather like a pup-pup-pup ponce." Billy was thinking aloud, as he did now and then.

"Really?" asked Ninian. "Curious, that Violet should have said that very thing only the other day." The little coincidence amused him. As Billy drove off he went on in a confidential tone, as if this frankness had created an intimacy, "Will you do something for me, without a word to anyone?"

"Yes, if I can," Billy said.

"I have a young friend whom I don't wish to name," Ninian said. "There has been so much petty spite where she is concerned! But she is one of the most naturally gifted human beings I have ever met. And I'm no fool, Billy. Nothing seems to cause her difficulty. For example, she has not had a great experience of painting so far, yet she identified without the slightest hesitation a Dufy which was not even in a familiar mode. An original drawing of her own impressed Mary Taplin very much. Her ideas for Silverwood, just touches here and there, say an unexpected tree or plant, are delightful." Ninian spoke in the steady, passionless, reasonable way of a judge summing up. "Now, I have often thought what a beautiful voice she has. Worth training, Billy, worth training. What I want you to do, very kindly, is to introduce her to a professor in London and ask him to take her as a pupil."

"Pup-pup . . . rofessors," Billy said, "are two a pup-pup-pup pup-pup-pup farthing." Ninian's words had touched off a signal of alarm. William Box's life was given up to music in the first place and after that to the care and protection of beings gentle and inarticulate like himself. Gossip entered his ear and sank directly into his subconscious mind; but now in those tangled depths something was astir and, groping about for it, he vaguely sensed that it was disagreeable. "And h-h-how can I introduce anyone if you won't nun-nun name her?" he parried.

"You have a point there," Ninian conceded. "Sharp fellow, Billy. We must think about it. Together no doubt we shall find a way. But I am not just looking for 'a' professor. I want someone . . . well, really, I had thought of Gustave Reni."

"Gug-gug-gug?" All at once Billy was very much afraid. That Ninian who knew the world and the place of men like Reni in it should make this proposal, and in so collected a manner, was staggering enough. Taken together with the really outlandish way he had got himself up and a peculiar brightness of eye that Billy noticed only now, it must, the conductor reasoned, indicate a disturbed condition liable at any instant to become acute. The spire of the Cathedral looked a very long way off: weakly he pressed on the accelerator. The many painful groundless frights he suffered tickled his friends a great deal, but he had lived so long in his nightmare, walking the tight rope that music lent him over a gulf wherein a host of agonized little creatures screamed wordlessly up for help, that he looked for catastrophe round every corner. If those things could really happen, so in his estimation could anything else.

"She would have to be a judge-judge-judge . . . enius," he quavered.

"I think it possible that she may be," Ninian replied, with an easy confidence that merely increased the other man's alarm.

But while the upper and conscious part of Billy's mind was anxiously picturing the forms that Ninian's derangement might take, the lower submerged one continued to stir and heave and labour until, with a last effort, it threw up a message so fantastic that his terrors were left by the way. "You don't mean to tell me," he exclaimed with rare fluency, "that you have Miss Fellowe in mind?"

"Sharp fellow, Billy!" Ninian said again. He supposed the conductor's guess to have proceeded naturally from his own last remark.

Billy laughed heartily.

"What is the joke?" Ninian asked in surprise. Then he burst out, "Box, surely you of all people will not join in this horrible meanness that is going on? It is pure jealousy. Jealousy of youth by the ageing, the most contemptible kind there is." Poor Billy was thirty-nine. "I think that never before have I felt so ashamed of *people* as in these last few weeks."

Billy checked himself and looked as solemn as he could. "S-s-sorry," he said. "I was thuh-thuh thinking of Reni's face." A gleam of merriment showed in his own as he thought of it again.

"Reni's face? What about Reni's face?" Ninian cried in a voice loud with temper.

"I was thuh-thuh-thuh . . . hinking of it," the conductor explained.

"Will you have the goodness to tell me why thinking of Reni's face should make you guffaw?" Ninian said, shaking a little.

"N-n-no," Billy bravely replied. "I wow-wow-wow won't, so there!"

Not another word was spoken until they reached their destination. Then La Touche said frigidly, "I will find my own way home," and slamming the car door he stalked away without taking leave or looking back. Billy sat methodically finding the places for the day in his prayer book and marking them with embroidered streamers; and then he walked into the Cathedral and joined wholeheartedly in a hymn. To find Ninian La Touche far madder than even he would have dreamed, had had a mysteriously calming effect on his nerves.

Ninian hurried through the cloisters to the Cathedral walk. To that long gravelled path, dusky with overarching boughs, he had brought many griefs and angers in his time, pacing up and down with the hiss of the foaming, eddying stream in his ears until tranquillity returned. He was appalled by Billy's defection. He had expected an eager interest, a wish to hear more, offers of help, and Billy had disappointed him as cruelly and bluntly as Mary Taplin had. What was this terrible thing in human beings that made them, even when gifted themselves, so resentful of distinction in others? How could a man at the top of his profession bar the way to a mere child without any resource of her own? Ninian did not pretend to knowledge of musical matters. When he saw Mercy's drawing he could state with authority that here was a talent of rare, exciting quality. For her voice, he depended only on a general instinct he had always had for excellence in whatever way it showed itself. He divined her capabilities without being able to formulate reasons. If after careful consideration Billy, or Reni himself, had told him that he was wrong he would have accepted it like a sensible man. Heaven above, the child had plenty of other strings to her bow! But to have the whole project laughed away with a crude, schoolboyish allusion to Reni's face . . . How little, Ninian sadly reflected, did one really know of any human being, even of those who were close and dear.

From the mighty Cathedral behind him came the growl of an organ and of voices muttering in sheepish rogation. There they went, Billy and all the others, mouthing their empty Sunday phrases, smug, odious, prepared to kill neighbour or friend. Revolted by their hypocrisy, Ninian thanked God that he was an atheist. Passing like this from a particular grief to the melancholy view of a whole helped to ease his mind; and with a few more turns up and down the walk, relishing in spite of himself the keen air of this first November morning as well as the brilliant foliage and delicious sound of water, he felt able to go on his way.

As he drew near to the little tearoom kept by Mercy's mother his heart began to thump and his legs to feel as if they were sliding from under him. His mouth grew dry as if it were filled with ash. How many years had gone by since last he had experienced anything like it! Indeed, he could remember the occasion itself, when as a youth of twenty-two he had stepped from a Venetian gondola onto the landing stage of the Princess Medallone's palace, for the first time visiting the renowned beauty alone. The memory came pouring back into his mind now, auguring well.

The building before him was trim and narrow as a doll's house, with neat pink bricks and white paint and the words "Close By" in flowing black letters above the door. A notice in the window said the establishment would remain open on Sunday and below this was stuck a grimy envelope with the words "Back soon!" scribbled on it. Enthralled, he peered through the windows into the tiny tearoom itself. The tables placed a few inches apart were neatly set, each with a vase of paper flowers and, by a happy idea, a lamp made from a Chianti bottle. The cups were turned upside down on their saucers, in order, he surmised, to keep the dust out until they should be used. On a counter at the back were a number of small teapots made, in the cleverest way, to look like Sealyham terriers; and in the window were cakes, iced with coffee or raspberry, coconut kisses, scones, mince pies and a row of pots that contained a clear red jelly. The wholesomeness of this jelly was somehow brought home to Ninian by the very fact that the pots were only three-quarters full. No machine-made stuff or machine-filled pot this, he told himself, but the work of an individual hand, a capable female hand that had, furthermore, written out, and stuck on, the labels outside.

He was greatly moved by what he saw. Not only the dainty charm of the place but what it stood for, the gallant resolution of the little enterprise, filled him with tenderness. What a wonderful woman this Mrs Fellowe must be, he thought, how she has toiled and battled and bled for her child! Craning his neck for a better view he found that the labels on the jelly said "Silverwood Crabapple" and this little attention, this naming of her jelly after the house where her daughter worked, pleased him very much. It made him wish that he could indeed have presented her with the Silverwood crabapples, but apparently there were none this year. Violet had commented on it the other day.

Now a window opened over his head and a cheery voice sang out, "Are you a lunch?" Looking upwards he saw a head protruding over the sill, its hair tied up in a gaily printed scarf and on its mature face a welcoming grin.

Ninian was disconcerted, as if he had been caught doing something foolish. "I'm really looking for Miss Mercy Fellowe," he replied on the spur of the moment.

"Don't tell me you're Ninian! Oh, I've heard such a lot about you!" the head exclaimed. It withdrew and the window banged shut. Presently it appeared in the tearoom, attached to a chubby figure clothed in red corduroy slacks and a black sweater that squeezed itself through the tables to the door.

"You'll join me in a coffee? I'm Olga, Mercy's mother." Ninian noted that the scarf on her head was printed with scenes of Paris by Night. "Mercy must have sneaked off with that beatnik. She is supposed to hold the fort on Sunday morning, while I tart myself up a bit. But here she isn't!" Mrs Fellowe pulled out a doll's chair for her visitor and smiled at him with her head on one side. "Will I do instead?" she asked, all teasing and sympathetic.

This then was Mumsie, of whom Mercy would

often speak. The horrifying thing about her was, he thought, that she so plainly was and could only be Mumsie. Here were the wide green eyes, not wavering adorably as if a kitten were trying to focus, but set like two little jellied gooseberries; the high Russian-style bones of the cheek had become two heavy knobs of flesh; the bright hair, cut in the manner favoured by the Garbo fans of yore, was brighter now than seemed permissible and the small brown hand was coarse from work and stained by nicotine. He was looking—macabre thought!—at Mercy in twenty-five years' time.

"I mustn't intrude on you," he said. He was torn between a desire to flee and a morbid inclination to hear a little more. "I only wanted to ask if Miss Fellowe could come back tonight, and not in the morning," he said, conscious of its sounding thin. "I . . . there is rather a rush of work, suddenly."

"I daresay she can," Mrs Fellowe said, with something uncommonly like a wink. "She's spending too much time with this fellow. I don't meddle with her affairs," Mrs Fellowe explained with uncalled-for emphasis, "but I can't see this leading anywhere. Sit you down, and I'll make the coffee, nice real instant coffee, none of your messy old grounds."

Singing, she retired to a lair at the back of the premises while Ninian sat down on the tiny chair and pushed his legs awkwardly under the minuscule table. All idea of going away had vanished in a twinkling.

"I hope the young man is a suitable companion for her," he said, raising his voice above the splutter of Mrs Fellowe's stove.

"Well he calls himself a beatnik," she called back.

"He tells Mercy about art and life. He was reading her this book where it said people like him were like Christ. Mercy wants to catch up on her culture, she thinks you're terrific and Viola makes her feel inferior. And this Eva Bernstein keeps telling her she must get experience, so she can have mature relationships later on. This Eva Bernstein has had any number of mature relationships, and she says they are the highest human good. But I don't see it leading anywhere."

As Mrs Fellowe had promised, the coffee took no time at all to make and very soon the cups were all rattling again as she wedged herself in at the table beside her guest. As well as the soupy greyish liquid she had brewed there were a number of mince pies, and these she insisted on his consuming. "I may not be in Olimpia's class," she remarked with a toss of her head, "but I can bake."

Her pies were a novel experience for Ninian, a morsel of mincemeat being walled up in a pallid soggy crust fully half an inch thick. Yet he ate with a will, his inner turmoil leaving him unaware of the dangers he ran. His only thought was to draw Mrs Fellowe out and make her talk, but, while she prattled away without stopping, he could not keep her on the subject that interested him. She always harked back to Silverwood, to him, to "Viola," as she called her, to the servants: she had mentally laid hands on his life and transferred it to her own, so that he could almost see her tripping into it and out again, hands full. Her vulgarity disgusted him, he was grieved to think of Mercy chattering about him to her, he sensed the humiliation of prolonging this encounter and yet he stayed, gobbling pies, an old man in ridiculous clothes, unable for the life of him to rise and go.

"I think Poppy sounds fun," Mrs Fellowe said cosily. She felt very much at her ease and privately congratulated herself on her "hit" with this Ninian. Funny child, Mercy, she had never told her how gloomy and haggard he looked. The part that Ninian played in her meditations nowadays would have astonished him indeed. Often she wound up her surveys of accumulating bills and dwindling custom with the thought, "Ninian won't let us down" or "Ninian will see us through"; and in her dreams he uttered such delectable phrases as "You must allow me, little lady, to present you with a deep-freeze." The little lady had realized long ago from her daughter's innocent prattle that he was "smitten" and, at the very time when the child was dismally wondering what he thought of her, had decided he was "in the bag." Now and again she dreamed of a marriage, May and November stuff, that should end happily in divorce —for this she regarded as the culminating point of any matrimonial enterprise—and a good-hearted settlement. But should he prove to be no more than just another "dirty old man," well, Mercy would decide for herself how far she wanted to go and there were bound to be pickings. And now he sat before her in the flesh, knocking her pies back and visibly taken with her personality!

The thoughts darting about in her brain did not interrupt the flow of her speech. "Poppy's right to enjoy herself while she can," she asserted. "I'm no angel myself, come to that. And I'm sure we'll all be dead quite long enough."

"How very true," he said politely. He could endure no more and got up to take his leave, jarring all the cups again as he did so. Mrs Fellowe pressed him to stay for lunch, and for tea as well if he liked. On his declining she sent him off with a ringing "Byebye! God bless!" and a vigorous wave of the arm. Then, Blow! she thought, as he disappeared. Why hadn't she complained to him of the price this Tito charged for the crabapples? Fivepence was little enough, but he would have given them to her for nothing. He would probably have coughed up the cash on the spot. Blow!

With her pies lying doggo within him like so many time bombs, Ninian walked to the market place and took a cab for home. His face drawn and pale with the beret coquettishly mounted atop caught his eye in the driver's mirror and snatching the beret off he flung it out on the road. The driver's own eye, unquiet, now appeared in the little square of glass and Ninian glared at it until it withdrew in haste. His mind was churning wildly away once more. The interview with Mercy's terrible mother, far from putting him off as it ought to have done, had made him long to be with her all the more. He had seen what she was to become with time, but with time he would not be there to see. It was now that was infinitely precious, this day and a very few tomorrows, and it was now that she was running about with a beatnik. Whom could that awful woman have meant? There were no beatniks in this part of the country, indeed, none had ever been sighted nearer than Oxford. He would speak to her this evening. He would explain that the fatherly interest he took in her, the desire he had to see her develop her exceptional gifts and take her rightful place in the world, entitled him to know what she was up to. He would advise, very kindly and gently, against her seeing the beatnik again. He would tell her of his plans for her future and ask if she would like to go abroad, on business.

As he went into the house Violet hurried up with all kinds of trivial chatter. Manley was in bed, sulking and pretending to be ill. Olimpia had slipped into his bedroom and administered an injection before Violet had realized what was happening. There she had remained for over an hour, the door locked, while Manley's voice could be heard rising and falling, talking vehemently, passionately, in Italian. Tito had placed his ear to the door and then calmly walked off, saying that the Signore was a gentleman. Billy had taken the monkey for a walk and it had broken into the hothouse, causing fearful damage to plants and equipment. Sir Alfred Box had rung up from London to know if his brother William were there.

"And where have you been, I should like to know?" she asked, staring at his tweeds.

He smiled distractedly and went upstairs without a word. As he got to his room the pies gave a first agonizing intimation of what they had in store for him and he dropped helplessly into an armchair. Writhing and doubling up, he again rehearsed what he should say to Mercy on her return in the evening. He believed now that he understood her. Craving sympathy and appreciation, she had been only snubbed and laughed at. The unfeeling attitude of these dreary middle-aged people round him towards the defenceless, brilliant child had ended by driving her into the arms of a beatnik. They should change their tune or he would make them sorry. They presumed on long acquaintance and his own good nature to indulge in every kind of impertinence. They should recognize Mercy for what she was and accept her position in his scheme of things or he would drop them. Violet should mend her ways or they would have to make some new arrangement for living.

But now Mrs Fellowe's mince pies gave tongue again with ever mounting fervour until at last they were in full cry and even her daughter was forgotten. Gasping, Ninian made his way to the bell and frenziedly rang it. When Tito appeared, looking surprised and alarmed, he begged him to run and fetch la Signora as fast as ever he could. He feared that he was very, very gravely ill.

Eight

Mercy returned from the outing with her clever new friend richer for his views on life and art but poorer by thirty shillings. Something of the kind had happened at three out of their four meetings and she began to think that culture would ruin her. She was not even sure if the money was well invested, for all her clever friend had to say of the people she mentioned was that they were no bloody good. These summary dismissals awed but did help her. She would have a like flow of brilliant patter to store away in her mind and roll off later as her own. Ninian's belief in her, however mistaken, helped her to believe in herself and by hook or by crook she meant to keep it going. She dreamed of Miss La Touche converted, penitent and admiring. Besides, she had a natural childish yearning to bow down and adore and she longed to hear that the names fished up from Ninian's clever reviews and newspapers were proper objects for this. But, "That old tripe-hound? N.b.g.," was Leo's epitaph on Picasso, Euripides, Kodály, Braque, Isolowolotumba, Turgenev and indeed everyone, alive or dead, except somebody called Ron something.

He must, she recognized, be fearfully clever himself to be talking like that. But she was making little or no progress in cultural matters and her black satin dress was further away than ever. The second time he asked for money she had refused it, only to yield after all before the storm of his indignation. "Don't you *want* me to eat?" he had exclaimed, with a passion that frightened her. Sometimes she wished she dared drop him, or even knew how to do it. Their meeting had been of an idyllic simplicity. He had walked up to her in the High Street and said, "Hullo, I'm Leo. You work for Poppy's brother," and she had remembered seeing him that day in the grounds at Silverwood. With no more beating about the bush he had said, "Lend me half a dollar and I'll buy you a coffee." Narrowly scrutinizing the coin she offered, he had taken her arm and pushed her along the pavement before him like a wheelbarrow. She admired his manly directness and sitting beside him in the café had felt sophisticated and unconventional, like a woman in a book. She had loved telling Eva Bernstein about it afterwards and had been thrilled by Eva's advice and warnings. But by now he had had in all four pounds seventeen shillings and sixpence from her. He was bleeding her white and, like a thirsty mosquito, could not be shaken off.

To make things worse, sitting in Leo's unheated caravan on the towpath with the dank river mist pouring in at door and window had given her a chill. She had come home flushed and shivering, and Mrs Fellowe had sent her to bed with a hot bottle and a drink of aspirin, afterwards scribbling a postcard to Ninian to explain what had happened. She did this rather than telephone, it being an article of her faith that men should be kept on tenterhooks and because she liked to think of him vainly and restlessly watching for her daughter's return, pacing like a caged tiger up and down that great Chinese rug in the drawing room that Mercy liked, though she herself would have changed it tomorrow for a nice fitted self. She wouldn't give anyone a thank-you for Chinese rugs.

What really happened would have been a disappointment. Far from pacing up and down, Ninian lay in bed sipping tinctures and swallowing pills. Mrs Fellowe of course knew nothing of the havoc her pies had wrought and she had but a hazy idea of the man that Ninian was. There were things in his character that far shrewder, subtler women might not have suspected. Of these one was the positively maniacal attitude to his health. Even a mild indisposition would cause him the gravest anxiety, and the searing agony inflicted by Mrs Fellowe's short crust left him without a thought but for himself and his chances of survival. Every time Violet came into his room he demanded if she "oughtn't" to send for Dr Benn and he was much aggrieved when after demurring for one reason or another at last she told him roundly they could not disturb a doctor's Sunday rest for trifles.

"*Trifles*, Violet?" he moaned. "This isn't at all like you," which was the more severe of the only two censures he ever passed on her, the other being "really rather like you, dear Violet."

In fact, Violet had rung Dr Benn up already. In the weakness of pain the invalid had babbled freely of mince pies and coffee although he still had sufficient command of himself to say these had been consumed at a place known to them both and called "Ann's Pantry." She had given him the particular look, bright, beady, that always reminded him of a parrot their grandmother had kept and that he fancied was now becoming habitual; and, without a word, had hurried away to the telephone. The doctor was writing a play, his normal occupation on Sunday morning, and was not at all pleased. "At it again, eh?" he snapped, and put the receiver down without a word of either advice or sympathy. The patient had to lie there, a suffering and neglected man, until the pains went off by themselves.

After dinner Manley came to say goodbye, with a courtesy he did not show as a rule. The progress made with Olimpia, who had listened enthralled to his description of the villa while gently massaging the spot in his huge pink buttock where her needle had gone in, the two exquisite meals she had sent up as if in expiation of her crimes at breakfast, had combined to put him in rare good humour, deliciously spiced moreover with the thought of his treason. Hugging that thought, he bestirred himself to go upstairs and put his head round the door of Ninian's room; and he chuckled to see the invalid supine on the bed with eyes shut and arms folded on breast.

"You'll make a lovely corpse one of these days," he remarked. He could never resist these little quips and would describe himself as his own worst enemy, although people often said he was wrong in that. "Goodbye," he went on, "sorry I haven't seen more of you."

"No doubt you will come again, fairly soon," Ninian answered, without moving or opening his eyes.

The evening wore away and night came on without his even thinking to ask if Mercy had come. Mrs Fellowe's postcard, brought with other correspondence on his breakfast tray, astonished him deeply. For one thing she had signed it "Olga F." and he could not remember an Olga F. There was the Princess Olga Felinovsky, but she would have sent a letter. And, in any case, would the Princess write "Our lamblet is rather sorry for itself, chill and slight temp. Not to worry, but don't expect her for a whilekins"? And could that vulgar, blowsy writing be hers? Mystified, he turned the card over thinking that the picture on the other side, a view of Positano, perhaps, or something *kunsthistorisch*, might furnish a clue. An enormous lady in a tight red dress was bringing down a rolling pin crack on the head of a bald little man with a red nose. The little man had just pinned up a photograph of some beautiful actress, and a balloon proceeding from the large lady's mouth held the caption: "I'll give you 'stars'!!!"

Such manifestations of the folk mind always gave

Ninian La Touche a kind of vertigo: on these occasions the idea of belonging to the human race at all would make him quite giddy. He buried the card among the other letters, urgently, as a dog buries a bone. "Please ask the Signora to come here," he said to Tito, flitting about the room like a little ghost as he put a touch here and there.

But Tito said the Signora was in bed.

"In bed?" Ninian echoed, both surprised and annoyed. Violet never stayed in bed: no one but he ever stayed in bed.

"No si senta bene," Tito explained.

"Oh! Mi dispiace." It was really rather like dear Violet to be unwell for the first time in years on the very day that he meant to continue unwell himself. Now he supposed he would have to get up and entertain Billy. "Tell the Signorina Fellowe I shall be a little late this morning," he said.

"No is return, the Signorina," Tito replied, as he lightly nipped a fading flower from a bowl.

That was Mumsie's doing, no doubt: dear Mumsie must have forgotten to give his message the minute he was out of sight. But then he had a sudden chill inkling of the truth. Exhuming the postcard, he peered intently at the mark and thought, blurred though it was, it might be the name of the town. With growing horror he saw that the date and time were clear, and realized that only a local posting could have got here so fast. Olga F. was none other than Mumsie herself, terrible creatrix of pies and grim foreshadower of a Mercy yet to come! How dared she write to him in such a way and on a postcard—and what a postcard! And how terrible the news! He

106

tore the card to shreds, allowing the pieces to fall where they might, and Tito flew to pick them up, smiling fondly as at some wayward but delightful child.

"Take breakfast away, Tito, and tell Signor Box I am too ill to come down," Ninian directed.

It seemed that Billy too was fled and gone: he had taken fright at Sir Alfred's threat of reprisals and had sneaked away before sunup.

"The little Desdemona, she stay," Tito said, beaming. "Is like a baby with the Olimpia."

"Very well, then. I shall get up."

As he lay in his bath he could not free his mind of Mumsie: it clave to her, like a fly to sticky paper. He thought of her jellied-gooseberry eyes, her dreadful handwriting, her taut grubby trousers and wicked pastry. It was not enough that she had mentally seized his life and made it hers but she now had to come thrusting in, an actual horrid presence. How stupid of him, he thought now, how blind, how cruel even, to have imagined the slightest, most embryonic resemblance between Mumsie and her child! He rejected the idea of such a thing absolutely. Mercy took after her father, obviously a refined and talented man who had made a disastrous marriage in early life and died soon after from sheer disgust. Yes, poor little soul, that was it; and now she was ill with no one but that harpy to tend her, and heaven knew when he would see her again.

He decided to pay a morning call on Mary Taplin, pretending to himself there were points to settle in connection with her show. He wanted her to see that he held nothing against her for not perceiving

Mercy's gifts; and in truth, he was sure it had been due to a blind spot and not to malice or envy. When people failed to see something that was crystal clear to oneself it was all too easy to impute unworthy motives. It was even possible that the others, Violet, Manley, Billy, all were blind rather than uncharitable in this respect. He also badly needed Mary's warmth to comfort him and raise his spirits, and hoped she would not be painting today. Remember, he abjured himself, to call that jackanapes "Knox." Knox, Knox, Knox. As he drove down the winding lane to Mary's house he had a peculiar sense of going in the wrong direction. Until today he had always walked to it over the fields, and if he took the car it was to run the opposite way into town. But I am far from well, he thought, with a melancholy shake of his head: far from well. He must go quietly for a day or two, he must spare himself. With alacrity his mind sped back to his health and was on it still when he rang Mary's bell.

Oliver opened the door with a look on his face that said "You again!"

"Morning, Taplin," Ninian said pleasantly. He wondered why the man's face puckered up in that extraordinary way when he was spoken to. "Can I have a word with Mary?"

"I have sent her to bed," snapped Oliver. The surprise in the other man's face induced him to add grudgingly, "She is not well."

Mary unwell too! The world today was full of recumbent females, Ninian thought with vexation. "Could I see her for a moment or two," he persisted.

"There is so little time left; and my secretary, who sees to everything as a rule, is away."

"Oh, all right then." Oliver stood back and allowed Ninian to come in. "You can find your way up, I daresay," he said. "I'm going to make her some lemonade."

"But she can't abide lemonade," Ninian remarked, smiling. "Surely you know that?"

"I think I should know Mrs Knox's tastes," Oliver replied, turning white. "I happen to be her husband." Leaving Ninian to ponder the mysterious truth of these words he stalked away to the kitchen and slammed the door. Almost immediately afterwards came the sound of breaking china, followed by a low, thrilling cry of despair.

Ninian pulled the knotted cord that hung through a slot in the door to the stairway. Nothing happened, and he pulled again and again until the latch lifted and the door swung out towards him, creaking loudly. As he mounted the first stair his head came, as always, into violent collision with the lintel and an icy draught hurried past his ears, whistling as if overjoyed to get out and into the only warm room. I must not stay long, he thought. On both sides of the stair hung terrible water-colours by Oliver's mother, and Ninian wondered again how Mary could endure them. He stumbled, as usual, at the point where the staircase abruptly wheeled and set off in another direction, missed his footing on the famous stair that, for some reason, was two inches shallower than the others, and hit his skull another ringing blow on the lintel at the top. Why, he thought bitterly, will peo-

ple do these things? Why take hold of a mill, useful
and respected, and turn it into an instrument of
torture? Under his foot the worm-eaten boards of
the floor groaned as if in agreement.

"Nothing infectious, I hope?" he said, pausing on
the threshold of Mary's bedroom.

"No, no," she said in her warm sweet voice, without looking up from what she did.

There was nothing the matter with her at all. She
had recently finished the last painting for her London show and was lazing for a while before beginning to work again; and Oliver had invented an indisposition for her to make himself important. Obediently she had retired to bed and undergone without a murmur the rigours of his attention, but only
half an hour since an idea had come to her, she had
seized block and pencil and now, propped up by a
number of pillows and cushions, was furiously sketching away, completely lost to everything round her.

"I see you are busy," Ninian said, coming into the
room. "Shall I go away?"

"No, no," she said again. She glanced up and without seeing him smiled in his direction. Then she
went on drawing.

"Are you glad to see me?" he asked, sitting down,
with a touch of anxiety in the playfulness.

"No, no," she said as before, smiling up for a moment.

"Mary!" There was such pain in his voice that she
looked up again and gave a little gasp of surprise.
"I never saw you come in, Ninian," she exclaimed.
"How long have you been there?" But even while
she was speaking her eyes veiled over and wandered

away to her sketch. In a moment she had resumed her work.

"Darling!" Oliver's voice, strangely lugubrious, came up the stairs. "Darling, where are the lemons?"

"In the lemon basket," Mary called back.

"Thank you, darling."

"I am not going to interrupt you," Ninian promised, "but I did want to make sure there were no feelings about the other night. I mean, about Mercy's talent," he explained, for Mary looked as if she were not following.

"Why, I should think not!" she replied. She added in a dreamy, distant voice that yet was kind and motherly, "You'll get over all this in time. It's only your age." She drew rapidly, smiling to herself. "I'm really surprised it never happened before," she said. Now she held out the block at arm's length and studied it through half-closed eyes. "Ah, that's what's wrong."

"Darling!" Oliver howled up. "Darling, where's the sugar?"

"In the sugar bowl," she answered. "Of course," she went on somniloquently, "one is sorry to see you being such a fearful ass. But most men do it sooner or later."

"Mary!" The fury in Ninian's voice surprised himself. "I see you are just like all the others," he cried. "Vulgar and petty and . . . and bornée!"

"That's it," she murmured, drawing busily. "But, Ninian, in time it will pass. It is a bore for Violet now, but it really will pass." She held her drawing out again and frowned at it. "It's odd how the quiet ones always go craziest," she said with her fat chuckle.

111

"I am going, Mary," Ninian said, rising to his feet in passion. "I shall not stay here a moment longer. I shall leave at once."

"Darling! Darling, where's the sugar bowl?"

"If you must you must," Mary agreed. "Thank you very much for coming. It has been so lovely to see you."

"Where's the sugar bowl, darling?"

"I wish you'd take that halfwit along as well," Mary observed, vaguely smiling at him as he stood before her and trembled with anger. Then she went back to her drawing as if she were all alone in the world.

Ninian strode to the door, flung it back and beat his head against the doorway. He stamped along the corridor like a raging child, missing his footing at the end of the stairs and coasted the remainder of the way down, fetching up against the door at the end with a thud that brought Oliver, in shirtsleeves and flowered apron, hurrying from the kitchen.

"Are you all right?" he said. He did not sound as if he cared, but the truculence was gone and in his eyes was a look of dread.

"No," Ninian said between his teeth.

"Nor am I," Oliver said. He hesitated, but his trouble had to come out. "I've broken her Toby jug," he whispered.

"She had no business with a Toby jug," Ninian replied, rising from the floor without even a glance in Oliver's direction. "Don't worry, I'll let myself out." Toby jug indeed! Mary's appalling tastes had always astonished him, for he inclined to think that artists were aesthetes like himself with a little knack for expression added on. Except for her own magnificent gift, she was a Philistine. He remembered how, meeting her years ago in Florence, he had been both shocked and entertained by her refusal to go to the galleries even once. "I don't want to look at other people's things," was her explanation. He had suggested that some of the things were rather good, and she had said, "Oh, yes," as if that had nothing to do with it.

Now he understood her attitude to Mercy's drawing. She not only lacked the discernment to evaluate it but was too self-engrossed even to look at it carefully. As for her vulgar comments about himself, they merely showed that she saw things with the dull stupid eyes of the world. They put her on a level with Mumsie. It would be a long time, he thought, guiding the car between the tall frost-nipped hedges, before he drove this way again. He had been as fond of Mary as of Billy Box; and now both of them henceforth should be as strangers.

Nine

By the time he reached home his head was throbbing painfully from all the mishaps at the mill. The thought came to him that very likely he had concussion. Providentially, Dr Benn's jeep stood in the drive and the doctor himself was just tripping down the steps, bag in hand. There was something in his face that Ninian took to be vexation at not finding him in and he hurried forward at once to explain and apologize.

"Benn, I'm so sorry," he cried. "I had no idea you were coming. Violet said nothing or I should have stayed in bed."

"I am attending Miss La Touche," the doctor answered.

"Oh!" Ninian was both relieved and slightly put out. "Nothing wrong, I hope," he said mechanically.

"I am not to discuss it," Benn said with a sharp look.

"I am very glad indeed you are here," Ninian went on. "Have you a few minutes to spare? Because I fear I have concussion." With eyes kindling, he was about to launch into the story of his case when the doctor wearily held up a little hand.

"La Touche, you must spare me," he said. "As I've told you before, you will bury us all. If you can control these freakish appetites. You are as strong as a bull. As two bulls."

Ninian was angered by this negligent attitude. "Concussion, Benn, hang it all," he argued passionately, "concussion . . ." but the doctor firmly raised his hand again.

"Spare me," he repeated, trotting briskly on. He vaulted into his jeep without opening the door, a practice which he said kept him fit although he was forever tearing and spraining things through it. "I've got twins coming in half an hour," he called out, rubbing his wrist before he started the engine. "And you have a visitor. Look after Miss La Touche. And, *for God's sake,* control yourself at lunch." Then he drove away.

Another visitor! It was really too bad. Ninian raised a hand to his aching temples. Was Silverwood a museum that people streamed in and out all day without invitation. He hoped it was not Sir Alfred, come hotfoot from Oxford to claim and remove his monkey. Olimpia's ululations would make his head a hundred times worse. But Tito told him, shrugging and grimacing, that a stranger had come, young, dirty, a savage, a Neapolitan almost, and would not go away. He had shown him finally into the bailiff's office beside the pantry and the intruder had broken forth, had strayed through the house as if he owned it, opening doors and peering into rooms. He had filled his pockets with fruit from a bowl in the dining room. "Proprio napolitano!" Tito repeated with indignation. He was in the drawing room at present, lying on the sofa in his dirty clothes and shoes.

Mr. Piper did not get up as the master of the house came in. Formality was never much to his liking and the portable radio on his diaphragm restricted his movement. His only greeting was a jerk of the oily head and the remark, "I've a bone to pick with you." He was dirtier than ever and his clothes had the look of garments seldom taken off; but his assurance was unimpaired.

"Please turn that thing off," Ninian said, holding his brow. All at once aeroplanes had begun to bang and roar about the sky: he knew it was the routine morning exercise, and yet he almost felt that they were the familiar spirits of this odious youth.

"I've a bone to pick with you," Mr Piper said again, ignoring the request. "Last time I saw you, you told me there were mastiffs in the ground. Mercy says there aren't any mastiffs, only a coupla Siamese cats or so belonging to the old girl. I demand an explanation," he finished haughtily.

Ninian dropped into a chair without a word and looked at him in disgust. When Mumsie spoke of Mercy and the beatnik and he had speculated so long and so anxiously as to who it might be, the name of

116

this Caliban had never even crossed his mind. How could she, he thought, taking in the low brow and wolfish eyes, the black fingernails and greasy collar, with all allowances for youth and inexperience and Mumsie, how could she bear him near her?

"Well?" said Mr Piper sharply. The repugnance in Ninian's face galled his proud spirit. "Did you hear what I said? I demand an explanation."

There were women who went in for freaks and monsters and hunchbacks. . . . "How did you come to be with Miss Fellowe?" he asked slowly, as if the words were dragged from him.

"I was educating her," Mr Piper disclosed. Something in Ninian's face piqued him again. "All right! She hadn't heard of Ron Novak, 'fore she met me. She didn't know what a status symbol was, or a father figure. You don't know who I am. My tragedy is, no one will ever know who I am. Cos I don't publish. And why don't I publish?" shouted Mr Piper in a sudden frenzy, actually turning the wireless down and half sitting up.

Ninian did not reply, but looked at him and shuddered.

"Why don't I publish?" Mr Piper proceeded with indescribable bitterness. "Do you, or do you not, want to know why I don't? Hell, I'm going to tell you. It's cos Ron Novak has said all I want to say. He got in first, and he sells ten thousand." With this the frustrated genius fell back on the sofa, spent, and turned the wireless up again.

"If you have any real purpose in coming here, please tell me what it is," Ninian said impatiently, with a glance at his watch. "And could you, without inconveniencing yourself, take your shoes off the sofa?"

Mr Piper complied with this request to the extent of kicking his shoes off and replacing his grimy, sockless feet on the sofa arm. "I've got to eat," he stated, with the air of a man certain of finding agreement. "And Poppy's turned close, on account of that Guy. If you ask her for anything now, she says she's a Zen Buddhist and money isn't real. She says the only real thing is love. I tell her, you try and eat it."

"My half-sister's activities concern nobody here," Ninian said angrily.

"Zen Buddhist my fanny!" Mr Piper mumbled, engrossed in his own thoughts. "She's going mean, like they do. And all through that Guy."

The indirect approach was clearly a waste of time. "I wish you'd hop it," said the reluctant host, holding his brow.

"You don't like me!" Piper now exclaimed, staring, as if the idea bewildered him. He fumbled in a pocket and brought out a banana which he peeled and ate, literally like a pig, with singular marshy noises within his jaws and scraps of the fruit falling from them. Then he leaned over to the little table beside him and festooned the banana skin round the neck of a jade buffalo of the Ming period. The action was mirrored over and over again in the ancient looking glass and other reflecting surfaces in which the room abounded, so that it appeared to be full of Mr Pipers, seen from every angle and all making themselves thoroughly at home. Ninian had a sudden lunatic vision of Silverwood's future as a national park of culture and repose for hordes of Pipers as yet unborn. I must get an heir, he thought urgently, as if making a memo for the tasks of that afternoon. A solid flesh-and-blood heir would have to be found, without delay. There was no depending on Poppy's daughter Isabel, who, understandably, had declared she should take the veil the instant she came of age.

"Go away," he snapped, glaring at the vandal, who now was rolling himself a cigarette.

Mr Piper's face suddenly cleared, like the face of a man who solves a problem that long has nagged him. "I know why you don't like me!" he crowed.

Ninian got up and took a step towards the door. "Come along and I'll show you out."

Mr Piper went so far as to turn his wireless off but made no other move. He lay there blowing wreaths of smoke and grinning up at the older man with eyes half closed. "You don't like me cos I'm educating Mercy!" A triumphant grin accompanied these words. "But she wants me to educate her. She asked me to. And why?" He leered up as if Ninian were hanging on his words rather than frowning at him in irritation. "Why does any female want education?" he asked, hooking his thumbs in the front of his coat in a judical kind of way. "Because she's sweet on a fellow that's got it, of course." Noting with satisfaction a flicker of response, he shut his eyes and puffed at his cigarette. "Not my type," he mused. "Too green and skinny. And I like 'em rich. Funny how rich women always attract me. What's more, I *stay* attracted. With the others, three goes are my limit. Funny." For a moment or two he pondered the mysteries of his temperament in silence. Then he opened his eyes and slowly got up, the cigarette stuck

119

on his lower lip and the wireless under his arm, and worked his feet into his shoes again. "So you don't want me to eat, eh?" he cried with renewed bitterness.

Ninian stood there irresolute, torn between the desire to be rid of the lout and the longing to hear Mercy spoken of, no matter by whom. Now the door opened and Violet came in, accompanied by one of her Siamese cats, creatures that he could not abide and rigorously excluded from parts of the house used by him. For Violet coolly to usher one into the drawing room was a declaration of independence, if not of war. It was on a par with her feeling unwell and remaining in bed. Good heavens, these women! he thought with sudden fury, thinking of Mary's impertinences earlier on. Violet took Piper in with the sardonic, parrot's look that he was beginning to find intolerable and turned at once to go.

"Violet!" he called loudly. "Just a minute! I want to introduce Mr Piper to you. My sister, Miss La Touche."

"How do you do?" Violet said, moving towards the door.

"Mr Piper is an interesting young writer," Ninian shouted, as if trying to gain the ear of an unruly meeting.

"I don't know his work, I am ashamed to say," Violet returned, smiling dangerously, with her hand on the doorknob.

"It is not yet published."

"Then there is a treat in store for us. Come, Jin-go!" Her careful pronunciation of Jingo's name was a pedantry that always annoyed her brother.

Jingo streaked across to the sofa where Mr Piper had lain and sank his sabre-sharp claws in its cover, his blue eyes madly blazing; and Mr Piper skipped aside with a cry of fear.

"Come, Jin-go!"

Jingo rushed to a window and scaled one of the great velvet curtains, looking crazily over his shoulder at the room below and howling like a fiend.

"Out of control," Violet remarked with complacence.

"Mr Piper will lunch with us," her brother burst out. "Perhaps you would tell the kitchen."

"Perhaps you would," was her answer. "I don't think I should dare."

Everyone appeared to have taken sudden leave of his senses today, Tito as well as Violet and Mary. Was Ninian La Touche, the master of Silverwood, entitled to entertain whom he pleased or was he not? On hearing that Mr Piper would stay to luncheon Tito had the effrontery to demur. "Is nothing to eat, is Monday," he kept saying and at last walked off while Ninian was still speaking. With the bunched fingers of his right hand he made the gesture, as if furiously scratching his throat, by which Italians express disgust or rage. Ninian decided to walk the visitor round the garden while they waited for the meal: it was one thing to invite him as a tease for Violet and quite another to endure thirty-five more minutes of him indoors and tête-à-tête.

Mr Piper would not be impressed and disparaged all he saw, although he smiled to see the huge chrysanthemum heads lolling on the ground where Desdemona had left them, and he laughed aloud at the mishap to McCardle. The gardener was just back at work after the pleurisy, and had come on the scene and viewed the damage to his exhibition blooms only a short time before themselves. Now with eyes shut and a foot bracing him against the invisible tree, he hauled on the unseen rope from which his employer dangled with an extraordinary fervour: until all at once either his foot skidded on the slippery bark or the rope must have snapped under Ninian's weight and he found himself sprawled on his back. There he remained, staring up into the sky and uttering a stream of objurgations in Border Scots, while Mr Piper laughed, a genuine, heartfelt, almost childlike laugh that made him more inhuman still.

"I reckon you're all barmy up here," he said. "Barmy as Poppy. Things run in families." He walked on chuckling.

Violet did not appear at luncheon, so that her brother's blow fell on space. Mr Piper ate eagerly, with the swampy gurgles and squelches Ninian had noted before, and apparently heard none of his host's conversation. Tito waited on them with loathing in his face and, once the dessert was on the table, went so far as to walk out without asking permission and leave the door open. Ninian chose to overlook this gothic behaviour, rashly, for as Mr Piper was about to help himself to grapes a little hairy skinny arm shot over his shoulder and whipped the bunch away.

"Mother!" he screamed. Perched on the chair back, Desdemona muttered crossly and dealt him a box on the ear. "Mother!" he screamed again, upsetting a glass of wine as he leaped to his feet: "Oh, mother!" Ninian shut his eyes and rang the bell.

"Remove that ape," he said icily with eyes still shut when he heard Tito come in.

"Sisignore," said Tito in his gentle voice, and smiling broadly he took the monkey up as she capered blithely about the table and, murmuring endearments, carried her off, while she nestled against his shoulder and munched her grapes. As the door closed behind them Ninian opened his eyes, to find Mr Piper shakily filling his glass again from the decanter.

"I wasn't afraid," Mr Piper said with truculence. "Don't go thinking I was."

"Of course not," Ninian replied. "Have you had quite enough? I will run you back to your caravan if so."

"You still don't like me," Mr Piper commented, looking puzzled again. "Anyone would have been a bit jumpy. This place is a soddy zoo. First it's wild cats, then it's chimpanzees. I'm not going to sit there heroic like an old Etonian with a perishing chimpanzee tearing my ears off."

"Quite right," Ninian said. "I'll go and get the car out."

"No rest, no peace, movement all the time," Mr Piper complained. "I like to be urged to stay. Is it Mercy again? I told you, she's not my type, Isabel's my type. Apart from her money. But that Mercy, I reckon she's sweet on you."

These few words had an extraordinary effect on Ninian. He did not know if they were true but the mere fact of their being spoken transformed the world: a world that, until then, had seemed more and more like a vast unsuitably converted structure where a man forever banged his head, and now basked in the warmth of giant sunbeams in the golden light of which danced little specks of dust like Mumsie and Violet and Mr Piper, at their own sweet will and with room for all. He smiled at Mr Piper. He looked at Mr Piper more closely than he ever had done before. He saw among other things that his hands, though grimy, were small and nicely shaped. Ninian always declared that hands were more indicative of character than any other feature: his own were beautiful. He smiled again and said, "What utter nonsense."

"Fact," Mr Piper said. "Girls like Mercy always kick off with a father figure. But go easy," he added, putting on his judicial air, "my guess is, she is not yet sexually awakened."

"The things young people say!" said Mr La Touche benignly.

He repeated his offer of a lift to Mr Piper's caravan and suggested that they first go for a drive as the afternoon was so fine. Mr Piper did not mind if he did and asked to be called Leo. His eyes sparkled when he saw the La Touche Rolls and as they drove down the avenue he began thinking how best to broach the matter of his finances. It was all too clear that the blackmail, on Poppy's account, for which he had come equipped with photographs and documents was a cock that wouldn't fight. Mercy's thirty bob wouldn't last forever, money went nowhere nowadays, it was shocking. And he had got to eat. All these sordid considerations were forgotten when they turned into the road and began sailing through the beautiful autumn landscape.

"Hi!" cried Mr Piper then, clinging to the side, "you've got a passenger!"

"When I drive, I drive," Ninian gaily retorted. He accelerated and brought their speed up to seventy.

"Oh, mother!" shrieked the filial Mr Piper.

"How is she, by the way?" Ninian inquired with formal politeness. He enjoyed himself for a few moments trying to imagine Leo's mother and also Leo himself as a babe in arms. Then he accelerated. He wanted to go faster and still faster through the crisp silvery air, he was ready to whirl on forever in the company of this craven boy, his throbbing head was quite forgotten, he felt that he was speed itself. It gave him a wicked pleasure to see one so young, so formidable in his youth, clutching the seat and whimpering with fear. He accelerated again, humming.

"Ninety!" Leo moaned.

A policeman on a motor bicycle slipped, stealthy as a blackbird, from a hiding place in the hedge and came on after them.

"We're tailed!" Leo shouted in mingled hope and panic.

"This is a free country," was the inaccurate rejoinder, as Ninian put on yet more speed.

Leo buried his face in his hands.

"Come now, I'll give you a treat." Ninian turned the Rolls aside through a gateway with a coat of arms in stone above it and great wrought-iron gates standing hospitably open. Slowing down a little he went on up an avenue lined with ancient elms that opened out at last to reveal a big house, in front of

125

which stood a lady speaking vivaciously to a gaitered Bishop. This lady wore a hat like a pink lampshade which, combined with the deeper hue of the face beneath it, gave to her head the look of an enormous fuchsia flower rising superbly from a coat of silver fox.

"Tally ho!" Ninian bellowed at the top of his lungs, with a boy's voluptuous delight in burning his boats. "That is our Mrs Bentley," he confided to Leo. Mrs Bentley turned with astonishment written all over her large purple face while the Bishop, a man of very nice nature, looked eagerly about him for a view of the hunt. As if she were commander-in-chief and he executing a cavalry salute, Ninian now swept the motor car round her in a curve, beating out an impudent tattoo on the horn as he did so, and scorched down the avenue again, passing the policeman who was just coming up and who followed the spoor in disciplined calm, swept round Mrs Bentley in turn and roared down the avenue after him.

You'll be sorry for this, Ninian's real self felt obliged to remark. Shut up, he responded: she's sweet on me, she's sweet on me. "We were lucky to find Mrs Bently so visible," he confided to Mr Piper as he turned into the open road again and accelerated. "As a rule her peak is in cloud." Mr Piper, now apparently more dead than alive and slumped in the seat like a scarecrow, made no reply. The Rolls sped on, a silver bullet, with the mounted policeman grimly pursuing. " 'Io son la fanciulla la più lieta del Giappone,' " chanted Ninian in falsetto. "Do you care for *Madame Butterfly*?" he asked of the inert figure beside him. "Ah, but no. Don't tell me! I can see you are a Mozart man." Mr Piper gave a feeble groan. Now they had come to the river and Ninian regretfully slowed down as the car moved onto the bumpy towpath. When they reached the caravan Leo opened his eyes with a shuddering sigh and looked at his driver with horrifying malevolence.

"I'd *Madame Butterfly* you for half a dollar," he snarled. "I'm lucky to be alive."

"And that good fortune is also ours," Ninian courteously replied, bringing the Rolls to a standstill and leaning back with the happy, satisfied air of a man who has worked hard and well.

The policeman rode up, stopped his engine and advanced menacingly on foot, as he had often seen it on the films.

"You've done it," Mr Piper sneered. "It's the beak for this. And you supposed to be a swell!"

" 'Hilft es dann kein Weh und Ach'!" carolled Ninian gleefully. "But look yonder!" he cried, his voice broken with mirth. "Is this a trap? Are we done for? Doomed?"

The door of Mr Piper's sweet little Kosi-Karavan with its chintz curtains and fresh green paint had opened. Framed in it was a burly man in blue uniform and with a boxer's broken nose, with the heads of others just visible in the interior behind him. There was, for some reason, an utter lack of repose about the whole little scene.

"Oh, mother!" Mr Piper exclaimed once more, with a beautiful, a moving, sincerity. "Oh, stars! Oh, crumbs! Oh, mother!"

Ten

The ludicrous things she does! thought Violet, ardently kissing a sheet of paper to remove the surplus lipstick. The "she" was Mrs Cloud, of whom some extraordinary photographs had been taken from Leo Piper by the police and handed to Ninian by an amused chief constable. They showed her, clad in *cache-sexe* and spurred riding boots, cantering round a tiny floodlit arena, somewhere indoors, on a chubby white horse: here and there among the onlookers the hats of French sailors stood out. These pictures had baffled the La Touches completely. They had known nothing of an equestrian phase in Poppy's life. Ninian, with his art-historical training, was inclined to date them at about 1946, the year when

Poppy had been engaged by the Army Bureau of Current Affairs as lecturer to the troops in Hamburg; and this seemed to fit in with the feel the ambience had of a German night club. But it was impossible to be sure, and Mr Piper had declined to say anything except that he knew where the negatives were.

Grotesque! Violet thought again, shading an eyelid with green. But for the first time in many years she warmed a little to Poppy because of the effect the pictures had on her brother. When he looked at them or spoke of their half-sister he became for a while his old self. He condemned all those, but particularly the middle-aged, who made spectacles of themselves, he deplored the irresponsible and castigated the frivolous; and declared that people could not live for themselves alone but must consider their families and the community as a whole. These sentiments, uttered with refreshingly deep conviction, never failed to comfort Violet and reassure her; but then, in almost the next breath, he would make some wild remark that showed how utterly misleading they were.

Miss La Touche was dressing with more than her usual care. She was always beautifully turned out, and laughed at for it by the county, who mostly believed it was middle-class to look like anything but an ancient bag of potatoes. Today was the private view of Mary Taplin's exhibition and she was determined to make the best impression she could. The thought of a gallery *vernissage* without her brother to manage it, easily and delightfully as he always did, his fine head and handsome face standing out in even that distinguished gathering, alarmed her dreadfully. But Ninian had to appear in court on the charge of dangerous driving, and there was no knowing what time of day the case might be heard or if, after it, he would feel inclined to come on to the show.

Her blood ran cold at the thought that he might not, indeed, be at liberty to come should he wish to. True, to career through narrow country roads and lanes at a hundred miles an hour was eccentric rather than criminal and there had been no accident. Happily, too, Mrs Bentley was not to sit with the other magistrates when the case came before the Bench. Ever since the little encounter before her house she had unremittingly voiced her belief that Ninian was mad, bad and degenerate. A man capable of shouting "Tally ho!" at Mrs Bentley, she reasoned, and in front of her guest the Bishop, would hardly shrink from theft or receiving. Mrs Bentley put it to her hearers as men of the world, or as women of the world where more appropriate, that an association of that kind could not be an innocent one. La Touche was, mark her words, in the Piper affair up to the neck: La Touche was, depend on it, the brains and Piper the tool. La Touche might have set himself up in poor old Charley Hume's place at Silverwood but that did not make him any the less a foreigner and middle-class. You had only to look at the shape of his ears to know what his proclivities were likely to be. She was half inclined to suspect a touch of the tarbrush. All this and more she trumpeted round the county, often driving for miles in rough weather to do so, until the Chairman of the Bench had been forced to ask himself if she were really geared to find a calm and reasonable decision in Ninian's case. Mrs Bentley had always believed that no cooler brain than hers was available to English justice and she now fearlessly taxed the Chairman with being in Ninian's pay; but he stood firm, and the court was to consist of himself and two others, men and sportsmen, all three the owners of large powerful motor cars.

This was all very fortunate, but, poor Violet mused, the outlook was still shadowed. It was dreadful enough that Ninian should entertain this youth with the prison record at Silverwood, this crony of their detrimental half-sister and receiver of stolen goods, who had been lying low in a stolen caravan. It was appalling that they should have been driving about the country together immediately before the youth's arrest. All this had got into the London papers, mainly because the celebrated art dealer La Touche had been called to the preliminary hearing as witness, and it would, Violet knew, tickle their friends immensely. She imagined the ecstasy on Manley's face as he read of it, and shivered. But even worse than that was the astounding attitude of Ninian himself. He had gone to court wearing those garish tweeds and hatless. He had offered to go bail and when bail was refused had exclaimed that England was back to the days of the Star Chamber. Piper, he had informed the Court, was a young writer of great promise. He had further declared—he, Ninian, who so often made merry over the clichés of the time— that Piper's misdeeds were a "valid protest" against a rigid, decadent society in which his gifts could never ripen. After Leo had been led away to his dungeon he had given an interview to the local paper saying, among much else, that the world needed love, not law.

The Bench won't like it, Violet dismally thought, shading the second eye. Having finished work on her face she completed her dressing, with three Siamese cats swarming about her ankles, and placed on her head a hat that looked strangely like a fourth. She put on a mink coat, for now the weather had really turned and bushes, statues, follies, hedges, all wore an elderly look this morning under their crown of silver frost; and with dark foreboding went on her journey to London.

Reynolds the junior partner hurried up, his pleasant features marked by suffering, as she came into the gallery, which was already crowded.

"Oh, Violet, did you ever see such a mess in your life?"

There was indeed little to suggest that the Gallery La Touche was noted for its exquisitely tasteful hanging. The pictures had been placed anyhow regardless of size or colouring or subject, as a baby might arrange a heap of bricks.

"What has happened?" Violet asked, with her heart in her mouth.

"I hung them," Reynolds said. "Ninian always left the hanging to me: it has been my special work. Mary saw them and she approved. Yesterday Ninian bobs up—he hasn't been near us for weeks, as you know—with that Miss Fellowe and asks for her views. And he made me carry them out."

"I think you might have refused," Miss La Touche

quavered, as the magnitude of the disaster began to sink in. Through the luxuriant forest of feminine hats she glimpsed Hazelrigg, the most viperish critic in London, staring about him in bewilderment.

"I tried to: it was like attempting to stay the charge of a rhinoceros," Reynolds told her. "It was the first row we ever had. I think it was the first time I ever saw him angry. He was beside himself . . . rabid. He called me a Philistine and a Queen Victoria and a square."

"He is not really himself."

"What can a 'square' be?" Reynolds wondered. "Can he have meant 'queer'? Surely not."

"He has been using a lot of new words in the past few days," Violet said. "Ever since he came home with a number of books by Ron something. What is Mary going to say?"

"Don't!" said the young man with a shudder. They were both silent a moment, for it was well known that Mary had a lioness sleeping within her. Presently Reynolds said, "It might have been better if I had sent the pictures to Montevideo after all."

"It really might," Violet agreed. "And if we had all gone with them. Oh, Dick! You know, of course, where he is today?"

"My poor Violet."

Violet passed on, hoping that Mary perhaps would not come at all. She hated being looked at and introduced, and the remarks people made about her work made her feel actually unwell. For the moment her place was taken by Oliver, and very ably, as he thought. For Mary's sake he had put his inhibitions resolutely aside and was throwing himself heart and soul into the function of a master of ceremonies. He would bustle up to a complete stranger, rubbing his hands, and inquire, "Everything all right, sir?" in the ingratiating tone of a maître d'hôtel, or, coming on someone deep in a picture, would graciously remark, "One of my own favourites. I see you're a connoisseur." Every time the little red label went up he would skip over to the buyer, beat him on the back and roar, "That's what I like to see!" As he wove in and out of the little groups of people, leaving a wake of astonished faces behind him, his heart was full of quiet but intense happiness.

"Why can't I always be like this?" he thought with a pang.

"I don't think you should be here, Miss La Touche," said Dr Benn. "You know what I said."

"My brother was prevented from coming," Violet said, bowing as the nice man from *The Times* squeezed by.

"Eaten himself sick again, I suppose," the doctor remarked. "I still wish you had stayed at home."

Violet smiled. "What a delightful surprise to see you, though! I didn't think you cared for painting."

"I don't," he said. "Give me a camera every time. But this afternoon is one of the great occasions of the year," he went on, his face lighting up. "Otto Zuckermann is going to demonstrate his new little dodge with the prostate. So I thought I would look in, since I'm up. Now do please be off as soon as you can and get some rest. There's a dear lady." He glowered at a canvas. "What's that, eh? A dog's dinner?"

"Those are almond trees in flower at Agrigento."

"Give me a camera," the doctor said, "every single time. Here comes that sickening friend of yours. Goodbye."

" 'Wears yet a precious jewel in his head,' " Violet thought, for Manley's eyes were so bright with malice today that they did look almost fine.

"A good throng," he remarked. "And a first-rate show. That Venetian twilight study is the most beautiful thing I have seen for years. It is splendid. Exquisite."

Violet could not help liking him just a little, as he uttered these words. She clung to a superstition that everyone has good in him somewhere and when Manley was thrown up as an argument against it would say, shaken but steadfast, that perhaps they did not know all. To praise another's achievement so ungrudgingly was generous at any rate and her voice was friendlier than usual as she replied, "Yes, it is a triumph for Mary. And a well-deserved one."

"On dit that old Solly Goulbin means to come," Manley said. "If so, Mrs Taplin is made. He will buy the three costliest pictures, on principle. Then they will go into a cellar until he sells them for twice what he gave."

"Goulbin's house is full of pictures: papered with them."

"Fakes, every one. Tell me, Violet"—Manley's eyes grew even brighter—"do I discern the fine Italian hand of Miss Fellowe in the hanging of these?"

"There's nothing wrong with it, is there?" Violet saw with panic that Hazelrigg had paused for a chat with Topsy Stroude and that both were smiling. "Anyhow, I don't know." Now Hazelrigg was laughing outright.

"Viola, darling!" A young woman whom Violet could not place at all barred the way, narrowing her eyes in affected shortsightedness like a woman of the world. A mask of white paint covered her face, and her lips lay buried under lilac grease, while mascara hung so thickly about her lashes that they looked like small feathers as she fluttered them up and down. This phenomenon wore townish clothes that must have belonged to someone older and fatter and were not altogether clean; but the effect was improved by her buttonhole, a rare orchid from the banks of the Amazon. Violet noted the bloom with interest, as she had never before seen it anywhere but in the hothouse at Silverwood. "My dear Viola, isn't this all too too marvellous?" the stranger asked, swinging a row of artificial pearls in one boyish little hand with an air of sophistication.

Manley was quietly laughing.

"Isn't it?" Violet wondered who the impertinent little creature could possibly be.

"What a charming name 'Viola' is," the creature gushed. She smiled kindly at the other woman, her teeth yellow in the white face, as if trying to put her at her ease. "I do wish I were called 'Viola.'"

"So do I," said Violet, and Manley chuckled.

The creature seemed a little taken aback by this reply and faltered in her gallop; but soon enough came gamely on. "Figurez-vous, I find in these pictures more than a touch of Renoir," she said, suave and knowing this time.

136

Manley laughed heartily. "Do you indeed, Miss Fellowe?" he said. "But I am afraid that there is none."

"Miss Fellowe?" queried Violet. "Am I to understand that our Miss Fellowe lurks behind that striking façade?"

Miss Fellowe blushed under her paint with ghastly effect. Again she boggled, and again came pluckily on. "I find that there *is*, Mr Manning," she said, toying with her string of artificial pearls and ignoring Violet's rudeness with great finesse. "And Ninian agrees with me."

"Ninian, Miss Fellowe?" Violet's tone was icy.

Miss Fellowe came off her perch with a bump. "He asked me to, so there!" she burst out. She was furious with them both and with herself, because this little scene that she had rehearsed so carefully in front of her looking glass had gone awry, and because she could not keep the babyish quiver from her voice. "He took me out to lunch yesterday after I had rearranged the pictures for him, to Santorelli, and we had spaghetti, so he could feel like a poor young student again."

"He never was a poor young student," Violet mentioned.

"Well, that's what he said. And we had wine and I had some chicken and beans and trifle, and he said I should call him Ninian. And he asked if he should grow a beard. He said he'd do whatever I said," she wound up, swinging her pearls in a sad little attempt at dignity. "I am to give him my decision tonight."

Everything was spoiled, the exhibition, Eva Bernstein's beautiful clothes, the make-up that Eva said made her look thirty if a day, the pride of her new status with Mr La Touche and even the pleasure of the Piper affair, of knowing someone in prison. "Forgive me if I am not quite myself at present," she had said over and over again to imaginary sympathizers, touching her eyes with a morsel of lace, "but a dear, dear friend has just been sent to gaol." Now all the happiness of being grown-up and having an interesting responsible job and criminal friends and a rich admirer was gone, swept away by a few words from this cruel old woman! Her lips trembled under their greasy coating: so young, so lost and helpless, she felt in Violet's presence that she could not think how to get away, and stood there in her finery like a child dressed up for charades.

I'll never have a mature relationship at this rate, she thought miserably.

Violet solved for the time being the problem of Miss Fellowe by pretending that she did not exist. She stepped round her as if she had been a chair and with strained attention began to examine a picture that she already knew inside out. Reynolds came buffeting his way through the crowd towards her, in a highly nervous condition.

"Goulbin's on his way!" he panted. "Where's Mary got to?"

"I haven't seen her. I daresay she's decided not to come—you know how she hates all this."

"She's here—I saw her a minute ago. She must be found. Goulbin likes to meet the artists," Reynolds explained. "Then he can feel he has bought them as well as the pictures. She must be found, she must be found, Violet," he reiterated, and battled off through the seething mob again.

"I am so very glad for Mrs Taplin's sake," Manley said, simply and warmly. "Really good work seldom finds a financial reward. And Goulbin never haggles. I wonder, Violet, if in view of this great success, this —as you rightly say—well-deserved triumph . . ."— he hesitated, choosing his words with care—"well, is there perhaps a chance that Mrs Taplin might give me the *Venetian Twilight*?"

Violet was oddly relieved to find him, after all, running true to form.

"But why ever not, Manley?" she said. "I'm sure Mary would be delighted to give a five-hundred-guinea picture to someone she knows a little."

"Do you think so?" he asked eagerly. "I hoped you would say that."

Topsy Stroude was approaching Violet with the steady remorseless movement of an alligator. "How sad that Ninian couldn't be here," she lisped in her dear little voice. "Is he avoiding me? I don't at all mind him refusing to pay my bills. I shouldn't want to pay his." She had a habit of blinking rapidly all the time she spoke, as if the light were too strong to bear: people often thought of her as a nice shy little thing.

"He has gone to the country to grow a beard," Manley said.

"Manley!" Violet almost shrieked.

"Is that why the pictures are hung in that delightfully surrealist way?" Topsy proceeded, quivering in ecstasy like a hummingbird that is sipping nectar.

"Hazelrigg says, Reynolds got in a little man from Selfridges. Violet, my pet, is that a hat on your head, or Jingo?"

"Jin-go, of course." Violet was glancing about her with all the desperation of a cornered rat. "Have you seen Mary at all? Solly Goulbin is on his way here."

"My dear! Well done, you." Topsy spoke as if Solly Goulbin were about to fall into a skilfully dug bear pit. "But he's royalty! Shouldn't Ninian really be here, and let the beard go hang? And will a beard become him?"

"He had one once before," Violet said, and thought, But then he was nineteen.

"Emphasizing his virility, I thuppose." Topsy purred. "I don't believe all these horrid rumours about him and that boy in the caravan." Well pleased with this little exchange, she passed on. Violet turned very pale and leaned against the wall.

The hum of voices had grown steadily louder and louder as people poured into the gallery and, after giving the pictures a dutiful glance or two, settled down to chat with friends and acquaintances. Now there fell a sudden reverent hush as Mr Solomon Goulbin entered the gallery. The mere fact of being in the room with the possessor of all those millions made everyone there feel richer and more important himself: the mere fact of his coming gave the exhibition a cachet and a new higher status in the eyes of the world to Marry. He stood there, a wizened, shabby old man with a bald yellow skull poking out of his threadbare coat like a tortoise's head from its shell, looking steadily in front of him, noticing no one, making no sign, waiting for the crowd to give him place. Respectfully people backed away to leave a clearing round him and the three secretaries in attendance. Holding their breath they waited to see him, with the unerring instinct for which he was famed, move towards the picture with the highest price and point to it without a word, leaving a secretary to conclude the business while he moved on to the second highest, and then to the third. It was a ritual of the London art world that no one who witnessed it ever forgot.

Oliver decided to intervene. He had no idea who Mr Goulbin was and thought him a poor old man who needed his advice; and he hastened up to him, hop-skip, as if taking part in a Sir Roger de Coverley, and asked very kindly, "What can I do for you, sir?"

"Nozzing," Mr Goulbin said without looking at him.

"Well, upon my word!" Oliver exclaimed, his demon awake in an instant. "You're very civil, I must say." He looked at Mr Goulbin's frayed collar and stringy tie and sneered, "Manners cost nothing, my good fellow." Another gasp went up, with here and there a subdued chuckle mingling with it. "You may be unaware of the fact," Oliver continued loftily, "but I am not a flunky. I happen to be the artist's husband." He folded his arms impressively and glared at the offender.

Reynolds could be heard somewhere, whimpering like a puppy. Mr Goulbin went on staring ahead of him with his old beady eyes, as if he were alone in the universe.

"I think it more than likely," Oliver went on in the same lofty manner, "that you have come to the wrong address."

"Ach, so," said Mr Goulbin. Slowly he wheeled about and crept from the gallery at his old man's pace, followed by all three secretaries.

"Only way to treat such people." Oliver smiled to the room at large, rejoicing to see them nearly all smile back. It seemed to him he was developing by leaps and bounds: a year ago, he reflected, he could not have dealt with the nasty fellow half so adroitly.

Manley thought with bitterness, "I shall never get the *Venetian Twilight* now."

The crowd continued to stand and stare as if in a daze and it was some moments before even a low buzz of comment broke out. No one thought of looking at the pictures again. Something had happened of such enormity that it was impossible to pick up threads or conceive what should follow, so that when a sharp smell of burning became apparent and almost at once the cry of Fire! was raised there was something curiously appropriate and even satisfying about it.

Wisps of smoke drifted through the door and, roused to a sense of their danger, the people began behaving as people do in emergencies, some doing what might be expected of them, others quite the reverse. Manley bounded from the room with the verve of an antelope. Afterwards he said he was deliberately giving a lead in order to quell the panic but at the time he had all the appearance of a man in flight. Oliver sprang bravely to attention, waiting in the fine old tradition for the women to reach safety before he moved; although, as he was standing just inside the door, they found it a little difficult to get out. Topsy, cool as a cucumber, had taken the arm of a frightened old woman and was helping her towards the fire escape, comforting her as they went along. Reynolds was hurriedly taking the pictures off the wall without a thought for himself. Anyone who knew him would have expected that, but why, Violet thought, in the name of heaven should Miss Fellowe be helping him?

Really, disasters were too bad: fires, floods, shipwrecks were dislocating and confusing enough with people behaving out of character, and further, she wondered, leaning against the wall, why need the house go round and round even if it was on fire? She heard Dr Benn's voice a long way off saying, "Stand away, please. Stand away, thank you. This lady is in my care," and then she forgot everything for a while. Presently she was on the sofa in Reynolds' office with Dr Benn beside her and Reynolds and Mary having a quarrel nearby, keeping their voices low for the invalid's sake but saying awful things in them.

"Ninian shall smart for this," Mary was murmuring, and Reynolds whispered back, "You ought to be certified. They were selling like hot cakes." "You ought to be boiled alive," she replied gently, and Reynolds: "You and your cretinous husband between you have just about sunk the gallery."

"Be quiet," said the doctor severely. "Ah, dear Miss La Touche, you are with us again. I have sent out for something to settle you, and then I am going to drive you home myself."

"How very kind! But what about Zuckermann's demonstration?" Violet asked, trying to sit up.

Dr Benn looked wistful for a moment. Then, "Bother old Zuckermann," he said, and his homely face grew almost beautiful as he spoke. "The prostate isn't the only pebble on the beach."

Now everything melted into everything else and Violet knew no more until she heard Reynolds exclaiming in horror down the telephone, "But ten days! My God, Deakin, *ten days!*"

"What is happening?" she asked.

"You fainted, as I warned you you might," Dr Benn said gravely. "Oh, that. Ninian has been put in prison. Now, dear Miss La Touche, you must really try to relax." He began rubbing something into her temples.

Mary and Reynolds had taken up their quarrel again. They were circling a table like two angry dogs, so that no one could have decided who was chasing whom, on tiptoe.

"I have a very good mind to sue you," Mary breathed.

"You should be sued yourself," Reynolds muttered. "You should be in gaol with Ninian."

"Shut up, ass! Poor Violet."

"What on earth is wrong?" Violet wished to know.

"I have told you. And you will not rest, as I begged you to. Oh, that," said the doctor, with a glance at the sparring pair. "Mrs Taplin lit a pile of newspapers and raised the alarm to get the gallery cleared. She was apparently dissatisfied with the order in which the pictures were set out. Don't see myself how it could possibly matter. But apparently people were very vexed when the trick was discovered."

"Good heavens!" she said helplessly. "And Ninian is in prison!" she cried as the truth suddenly penetrated. "I had a foreboding of it this morning as I came up. But why? Why? What has he done?"

"Now I really cannot allow this," the doctor said firmly. "I forbid you to worry or, indeed, to think at all. Here's our physic, bravo! You will soon be as right as rain."

"Good heavens!" she said, taking the dose from his hand.

"Spineless gutless snake in the grass," Mary hissed.

"Over my dead body do you enter ever this gallery again," Reynolds softly made reply.

"Cretin. Lackey. Traitor."

Eleven

When Ninian set out for the court he had no idea of
what lay in store. Mr Deakin the solicitor had nerved
himself to beg that his client would dress quietly
and answer the Bench with relevance and respect.
Were these conditions observed, Mr Deakin was of
the opinion that his client would get off with a small
fine or even with none. Were they not observed, in
view of certain matters extraneous no doubt to the
case but inevitably present in the magistrates' minds,
Mr Deakin would prefer to express no opinion at all
as to what might happen. Ninian readily complied
with the first and had every intention of adhering to
the second.

Unhappily, as he stood in the well of the court

awaiting his turn he had a kind of vision. He seemed all at once to be looking at things with the fresh unclouded eyes of a child. Those three old men with their snowy hair and their faces red with drink ought not to sit in judgement on their fellow beings, he saw. There was something inherently wrong in the system that allowed it. How many times in the past had he himself picked the old Admiral off the floor, for example? And there the Admiral sat in a place of honour, mumbling in sententious agreement with the Chairman's platitudes.

The vision crystallized into intellectual convictions during the case immediately before his own. It concerned a shepherd accused of doings in connection with his flock such as are not uncommon in unspoiled rural areas, and all ladies were driven from the room while it lasted. The man clearly could not understand what the fuss was all about. "Us fooks 'em and us boogers 'em," was his own stalwart admission and he held his head high, as became an upholder of the dying tradition of English yeomanry. But not content with handing down the maximum sentence in its power the Bench felt called upon to make remarks as hypocritical as they were priggish. "The animal world must be protected from the likes of you. . . ." This from the Chairman, who was only happy when chasing, shooting, hooking or impaling some inoffensive little fellow-being! Why should not he rather stand in the dock and this honest shepherd with his ruddy countenance and clear eyes pass judgement on him? Were any of the flock complaining? No. And who was to care for them while their keeper was away? Why should the innocent suffer along with the guilty, and all of them through the mere prejudice and caprice of society?

These questions ran through Ninian's mind while the warders marched the shepherd away to the cells and the clerk called out his name. His promise to Mr Deakin was forgotten. When the Chairman, aware of his acquaintance with the Admiral, asked if he objected to the Bench as constituted he replied at once that he did indeed object to it, as to all other kinds of buffoonery. Mr Deakin looked up from his papers with his mouth open. Ninian refused to plead guilty as arranged, or to apologize, or to do anything but heckle and interrupt. With his suddenly lucid view of the world he saw that if it were dangerous for him to drive about at a hundred miles an hour it was equally so for the half-baked policeman on the motor bicycle behind: yet no one had challenged the latter and there he stood in the witness box, his hair glistening with brilliantine and a nauseating look of virtue on his face. It was the hand of society again, dead but still cruel. He persistently tried to make this important point but the Bench refused to hear and he grew angry with them. While Mr Deakin covered his eyes as if in prayer, he called the Chairman a blood-thirsty old ruffian and the Admiral a tedious old alcoholic. He did not know the third magistrate well enough to be able to call him anything. Vexed, embarrassed, amused, the Bench had a whispered consultation as to whether it might not be possible to remand him for a medical report; but reluctantly agreed that the charge was not weighty enough in itself and that there was nothing for it but to send him to prison without the option.

148

"It is indeed painful to see a man of your up-bringing and position come to this," the Chairman gravely told him, and the other magistrates growled and grunted.

"Oh, shut up, do," Ninian said.

Mr Deakin gave a little moan: he seemed more dead than alive.

As he sat in the Black Maria between the shepherd and a thief on their way to the county gaol, Ninian thought with a pang that now he would not be able to keep his appointment that evening with Mercy. He wondered if she would have heard of his plight or whether she would turn up at their meeting place and wait there, growing perhaps angry or miserable. It would be ten whole days before he could see her again, all through his own fault; and ten days, too, before he would know if she wanted him to grow a beard. He himself was partly in favour of it because the hair on his chin still grew dark, not white, and partly against, because his chin was good. The best thing, he thought, would be if he grew it now, regu-lations permitting. In ten days it would be sufficiently long to give her an idea of whether she would like it or not, and she would not have to see him at all in the first, unprepossessing stage. As he reflected on these matters, turning them over in his mind, weigh-ing this against that, he clasped his beautiful hands together and his face took on a serious, troubled look that moved the decent shepherd to compassion.

"Very sorry, sir, I'm sure," he said with rough kindness. "Us do be accustomed like, but it's rare hard on gentry. It don't seem natural, and that's a fact."

"Quiet, you," said a policeman through the wire grille.

The first meal Ninian ate in prison consisted of cocoa, porridge, bread and margarine. These were substances he had read about in books but never encountered, and they made him so unquestionably ill that he was carried to sick bay on a stretcher. A kind prison doctor saw no reason unduly to expedite his recovery, so that he was able to spend the whole period in bed, growing his beard and thinking of Mercy. He felt contented and at peace. One morning there came a long letter from Mr Piper, with a number of passages censored, to ask for sympathy, understanding and twenty pounds by return; and it gave him, absurdly, a boyish thrill to be able also to put a prison address on his reply. The chaplain visited, a sweet vague old man who was also honorary chaplain to the Bishop, and spoke earnestly about his way of life.

"Not a very handsome thing, you know, to shout 'Tally ho!' like that," he gently reproved him. "The Bishop drove hither and yon till dusk, looking for hounds. And the Bishop is a pretty busy man, I can tell you." Likewise, the Bishop was grieved that Mr and Miss La Touche never attended a place of worship, either locally or at the Cathedral. "No one asks you to believe anything, after all," the old chaplain coaxed him, "but it sets an example." He sat there smiling, his head trembling a little on his shoulders, and all at once appeared to mislay the thread of the conversation. "I should go to Australia when this is all over, my man, and start afresh," he said encouragingly, his old blue eyes kindling with a reformer's zeal. "The Bishop will gladly assist you with the fare, you may depend on it."

The idea of going to Australia as an outcast, helped by the Biship, added somehow to Ninian's sense of well-being. How strange it was, he thought, that lying here in a prison bed he should feel truly free at last after years and years of restraint! For the first time, too, he felt at home in the twentieth century. A short time ago the very thought of missing a gallery *vernissage* would have seemed quite monstrous: now it brought him only more relief and pleasure still. To listen to those parrot cries, to play up, to wait on tenterhooks for Goulbin's coming, to endure his brusqueries when he came—how had he ever endured it? He remembered with delight all the other things he would have had to do this week in London, had he been what was known as at liberty.

"What a lucky, lucky fellow I am," he murmured aloud; and a prisoner in the adjoining bed looked at him dazedly.

The welcome he got from the Italians on returning to Silverwood was rapturous. Tito had leaped to the conclusion that the offence was political and now revered his employer as a kind of Garibaldi. He ran down the front steps to greet him, repeatedly bowing and kissing his fingers, while Olimpia's cries and sobs and ejaculations rang tempestuously through the length and breadth of house and garden. Stupendous courage! A hero's patience! And the beard, how beautiful! Il Signore looked twenty years younger! One would say, a boy! And ah, the happiness of the Signore's safe return! Mrs Dimble looked at him with motherly interest. Even McCardle gave him a sour half-grin and sketched a movement as if to touch his cap.

Ninian was deeply moved by their good will and in consequence was all the more put out to find Violet's manner towards him cool. He had expected anxious enquiries for his health and startled comments on his beard: there were none. She was in the drawing room with all three Siamese cats about her, howling and clawing at the furniture, in conversation with a Mrs Cudliffe. At the sight of this lady, a rival of Mrs Bentley's, Ninian felt a rush of the old inner frenzy such as he had never known while in gaol. He realized that she had called this morning out of mischief, and also as a slap to Mrs Bentley, who was striving to unite the county in a boycott. All he wanted was a bath and a meal before he hastened in search of Mercy, and to sit down and talk to a visitor was almost beyond his power.

"A cousin of mine did time once," Mrs Cudliffe was saying. Her remarks were made in a kind of roar, a habit due to the fact that most of her discussions were held in the saddle. "Buggery, of course. In my young days, gentlemen never went in for anything else. Things are very different now."

"That must have been nice," Ninian said politely. Try as he would he could not keep his mind on what the woman said. Impatience to be gone burned in him like a physical pain: scraps and phrases only penetrated his mind as he sat there, chafing, a vision of two large green unsteady eyes before him. Would she be glad to see him again? But really glad? What would she think of his going to prison? Would she like him more for it? What had she been doing with herself these last ten days? Oh, he could not wait, he could not wait . . .

"Such an old sleepyhead," Mrs Cudliffe roared. "I thought he was goin' to be some use with the guns. But he lies about all day, lickin' his private parts."

"Indeed," said Violet. Despite all her years in the shires she had never got used to these modes of speech.

"Funny, how wrong you can be," Mrs Cudliffe went on. "I could have sworn he was the right stuff."

"What is his name?" Ninian asked, making an effort to appear interested.

"Rover," replied Mrs Cudliffe. "Unusual, eh?" She put her head back and bayed in amusement.

"Oh. Yes, yes . . . isn't it? I knew a Rover quite well, back in the thirties," Ninian said, with the over-eagerness of a guilty conscience. "Could it, I wonder, be the same one? A geologist?"

"No," said Mrs Cudliffe. "A Labrador."

Ninian was thinking of a hard little hand slowly guiding a pen across the pages and scattering lovely nonsense to the four winds as it went. "Ah, it must be another, then," he said in the same effusive tone. "Come to think of it," he said with a smile, rounding things off, "the geologist's name was Roper."

He fell into a dream and spoke no more, while Mrs Cudliffe looked at him, her mouth pursed in a soundless whistle, and Violet raised a glass of Madeira to her lips as if it had been a poison bowl.

After the simple arrangements of the prison hospital it was delicious to wallow in a hot bath, surrounded by gleaming white tiles and chromium fittings. He dressed with great care and lovingly fondled his beard, which now was nearly long enough to brush to a little point. Should he dye his hair to match? the contrast was strange. But the silkiness of his hair was one of its attractions, and dyeing would take it out. And it might be that Mercy would direct him to shave the beard off. Should he wear a blue silk shirt with the light grey suit, he wondered next, smiling into the looking glass at what he thought of as his "prison pallor," or the more conventional red-and-white-striped poplin? Yes: today he would be as orthodox in dress as could be. It would make his beard and his conversation all the more piquant.

The cat digs the square, he thought buoyantly. Or should it be, the square digs the cat? That was the kind of thing Mr Piper would know.

He had seen no newspapers in prison and Reynolds had not written to him, so that he was unaware of the happenings at the *vernissage*. His responses to them were as unpredictable as everything else about him these days, Violet thought. He had nothing but praise for Oliver's handling of Mr Goulbin, saying it was exactly what he had always wanted to do himself and had not dared; and that Oliver clearly had been misjudged and underprized. On the other hand, when Violet told him of her erstwhile favourite's method of clearing the gallery, he turned pale with fury.

"That woman goes too far!" he burst out. "She has lost the gallery its name, as well as hundreds and hundreds of pounds. These artists think of nobody but themselves."

"The pictures were so frightfully placed," Violet began, but he interrupted her.

"They were beautifully placed," he cried. "Do you know what's behind all this persecution? Feminine spite. Just because the child made a little slip over Montevideo. And jealousy. Because Mercy has a fresh young talent."

"You thought the world of Mary's own work once," Violet said.

"Oh, yes yes yes, it's very well, very well indeed, in its way."

"You thought the world of Mary, too."

"I was deceived in her," Ninian said. "Everyone can make a mistake. Poor Knox is much to be pitied."

"Perhaps. But Mary was not alone in her view of the hanging. Wait until you see what Hazelrigg wrote." With many others Hazelrigg had waited in the street to see the fire engines at work, and the discovery of the hoax had charged his pen with extraordinary venom.

"My dear Violet! This cat doesn't dig that square!" As he uttered these words Ninian looked infinitely pleased with himself; and he settled to his luncheon with excellent appetite.

As soon as the meal was over he got out the Rolls and, although the Bench had suspended his licence, drove with all speed to town. He parked the car in the Close, in the Bishop's parking lot, and hurried round to the tearoom. Mumsie was there, serving a poached egg on toast to a curate; otherwise not a soul was to be seen. The Silverwood crabapple jelly had not been sold, and the cakes too appeared to have been undisturbed since his previous call. Mumsie herself was just the same, in the tight red trousers and dusty black sweater, except that today she was looking haggard with worry.

At the sight of Mr La Touche, however, she brightened wonderfully.

"Oh, you naughty boy!" she sang. "You naughty sporty boy! And it's got a beard! Come in, don't be afraid. Olga likes naughty sporty boys."

"Is Mercy in?" he asked. He thought of the postcard and shivered.

" 'Fraid not. She's out and about with this Eccles," Mumsie said. Leering, "I won't do instead?" she asked, as she had done before.

"Eccles?" Again he felt that longing to flee, that inability to move.

"Organist at the Cathedral," Mumsie said, "and married. But there! You'll be taking her off, now you're out." She leered again. "Too busy to acknowledge my card?" she suggested. "Running about with that Piper! That was a lark and a half. We had the police in too."

"Pardon me for the interruption," the curate said, "but this egg is musty."

"Indeed!" Mumsie cried indignantly, as if he were somehow to blame for the fact. "Well, make the best of it, then, for it's the only one in the house."

"I'd sooner have sardines on toast, if you're agreeable," the curate pleaded.

"Would you now, Mr Fancy Pants," she riposted. "I'm to open a tin of sardines just for one, I suppose. Ha, yes. I daresay."

156

The curate placed a shilling on the table and with dignity left the establishment.

"And that's what goes into the Church these days!" Mumsie said, throwing her arms dramatically wide. "Tragic! No money, no connections. Well, where were we? Oh, yes. You'll want my lamblet back again now." The gooseberry jellies glinted at him with infernal understanding, then pounced on his overcoat. "That's a nice bit of stuff," she said. "You never got that at a jumble sale!" She was drawing near with the intention of feeling the material when her demeanour underwent a remarkable change. "Oh, my sweet Lord Jesus," she faltered, "here's Moby Dick!"

An enormous man strode into the little café, threw his hat on a table and shouted, "I'm sorry, ma'am! I'm sorry!"

"Give us a chance, Mr Starkie!" Mumsie was trembling all over like some frightened animal.

"You've had chances, ma'am! You've had chance after chance." Mr Starkie picked his hat up and dashed it down again for emphasis. "I *hate* doing this," he said delightedly, "but I have to."

"If only it was the fridge!" Mumsie groaned. "But the tables and chairs. I'm sunk without the tables and chairs. Oh, Ninian," she said, bursting into tears, "tell him to leave me the tables and chairs!"

Mr Starkie turned his great head in Ninian's direction and took him in with the deep, sad wisdom of a hire-purchase agent. "This gentleman," he said, "understands the world too well to interfere. This gentleman respects himself too well to push for-

157

ward. This gentleman prefers to be left out of what don't concern him and *if* it's all the same to you, ma'am, my time is valuable and it's thirty-one fifteen and six or the boys come in now. There," intoned Mr Starkie, gesticulating over his shoulder with a thumb like a banana, "waits the van." And he folded his arms with a triumphant smile.

"No, no. What is the trouble? Is it a payment of some kind?" Ninian felt as if he were moving in a new dimension altogether. "Perhaps it can be arranged," he said, more to end the scene than from goodness of heart.

"Oh, Ninian, if you would!" Mumsie clasped her hands and rolled the gooseberry jellies. "I've had such appalling luck this summer. Trouble is, I can't afford to advertize. Nobody knows about me." She was reviving fast.

Mr Starkie looked far from pleased, for he loved the intense emotions of a forced removal. "The gentleman probably has thirty-one pound fifteen shillings and sixpence in his pocket," he said. "I hope so, I do indeed, for nothing but cash down and on the table will suit. I hate to say it, I'm sure, but I have to. It's cash or nothing." And he smiled again, quite pleasantly.

"Couldn't you take a cheque?" Ninian said. "The banks are shut. My name is La Touche and I come from Silverwood."

"You tell me," Mr Starkie took him up sonorously, "that your name is La Touche and that you come from Silverwood. And you may well be right, for who is in a better position to know? But that don't help me. In my walk of life, sir, we learn hard truths about human nature. And it's cash or nothing."

"Can you wait a few minutes, then?" Ninian said. "While I go round to one of the tradespeople and cash a cheque there?"

Mr Starkie's huge face fell. "I will give you fifteen minutes," he said after a pause, drawing a watch from his pocket and swinging it in his hand. "And why do I give you only fifteen minutes? Because, sir, time is money and because, sir, it has been known for a gentleman to make a gesture like yours, particular in front of the gentle sex, and to walk out and be seen no more. While the other party waited on in empty hope."

"You have indeed poor a view of human nature," Ninian said, unable to keep from smiling.

"And I am seldom wrong, sir," Mr Starkie replied with satisfaction. "Seldom wrong. You might say, never."

"I must look sharp, then, so that I may prove you wrong for once." Ninian hurried towards the door, followed by a ringing "God bless you!" from Mumsie. Mr Starkie was heard to mutter that it was now three-fifteen and twenty-two seconds. Laughing, Ninian hastened onwards almost at a run, determined to frustrate Mr Starkie and enjoy his discomfiture. Mr Starkie clearly had the same hidebound cliché-ridden mentality as the Bench, which to confound was a duty as well as a pleasure. As he reached the end of the lane his name was shouted in a tone of authority mingled with deference and, turning, he saw a young policeman speeding towards him.

Through the gateway of the Close he caught a glimpse of another, who waited beside his Rolls. They had of course recognized it: they had of course known that he was not allowed to drive: they must know that he had been freed from gaol only that morning. He lost his head and began to run in earnest now, thinking that if he could only double into the High Street and get as far as his wine merchant the money could be sent round by messenger and himself lie doggo until the coast was clear. But the constable was the younger by thirty years and more and caught him up with ease.

"Very sorry indeed, sir," he said, avoiding the culprit's eye. The gasping Ninian noted that his breath came none the quicker for the little sprint. "But I'm afraid you'll have to come and speak to the Sergeant."

Other police were looking in their direction, prepared to intervene.

"You didn't ought to do it, sir," said the lad sorrowfully, as he guided Mr Ninian La Touche home to the police station. "You really didn't ought to do it."

Twelve

"Violet, I cannot endure this." Ninian spoke in a tone of piteous appeal.

They were sitting at luncheon together, one at each end of the long table. Formerly when they were alone Violet had always taken the head, with Ninian on her right-hand side. The three Siamese cats were in the room again, sniffing and howling, bounding lightly onto the table and off, threading their way among the dishes, raking the furniture with their murderous claws.

Violet said nothing but took a piece of beef from her plate and gave it to Jingo.

"Violet, please!" he cried. "Don't encourage them. How can you, how *can* you, bear them near you?"

"I must have something near me," Violet said. She gave a morsel of beef to Pibun. Jingo flew at him, upsetting the mustard pot, and the dining room resounded with feline hate. Taikun sat and coolly watched the fight, his mad blue eyes blazing and his tail switching from side to side.

"They are demons," Ninian said with a shudder.

"They are marvellous creatures," Violet said, unmoved, raising her voice above the din. "They are millions of years old, each one. They have forgotten a thousand times more than we shall ever know. But what is the use of talking? We have said all this before. One is a cat person or one is not."

"You might have a little pity for me," Ninian said, raising his voice too and putting a hand to his temple. "You know I have to appear in court this afternoon."

"You have to appear in court most afternoons," his sister replied.

This was an exaggeration, for Ninian had last appeared in court three weeks ago. He had then been fined fifty pounds for the offence of driving without a licence, the Bench taking a particularly grave view since it occurred on the heels of his release from gaol. Now he was to be charged with drinking on licensed premises after hours. He had never been in a public house in his life before the Saturday evening that this one was raided. He was radiantly happy and blithe just then: he had kissed Mercy on the top of her head as she sat typing, and she apparently had not disliked it; and he had astounded the dinner table, which included Manley and a nice man from Sotheby's, by saying he would visit The Fish That

Jumped after the meal and calling for volunteers to accompany him. He met with no response and went alone, to find a musical evening in progress with a youth playing an accordion and the honest farmers, yokels and bargees raising their voices in song. Captivated, he had joined in, sung and swallowed pints of beer with the rest and when the police rushed the bar soon after midnight had rebuked them for spoiling the fun with such warmth that he was all but taken up for obstruction.

Mr Deakin had handed the case on to his partner, Mr Garrish. The firm of Deakin, Deakin, Garrish and Deakin was not accustomed to clients being found in low taverns or arraigned in one dock with individuals named Gann, Pincher, Watt, Hilcock and Sheepwash. Only once before had a similar misfortune befallen them, and that had been in the eighteenth century. Nor was Mr Deakin, an elderly man with something wrong with his heart, prepared to undergo another experience like Ninian's first brush with the Bench.

"A new client, Mr Garrish," he said, dolefully shaking his head. Ninian had been consulting him for barely twenty years. "Curious, how seldom any good comes of a new client."

"Will you drive me in?" Ninian shouted. Taikun had now decided to intervene on Jingo's side and the hubbub was deafening.

"I am sorry, I cannot," Violet screamed back. "Sir Alfred Box is coming to fetch Desdemona away."

She feared that there would be serious trouble, not from Sir Alfred, whose very pleasant letter strangely contrasted with the gruff baritone voice that had threatened and bullied them over the telephone, but from Olimpia. Sir Alfred had been too busy to come before, and in all the brilliant team of scientists he led only he was able to manage a monkey; so that Desdemona by now was a member of the Ricci family and no one had dared to breathe a word of the parting that lay ahead. The grief of the little monkey's loss would add itself to that of the little sister's in Olimpia's warm and fecund heart, resulting in such transports of woe as made the mind stagger to contemplate.

"Then how shall I get there?" Ninian bawled.

"By taxi," Violet screamed. "Or bus."

"Bus, Violet? Are you mad?"

Taikun came scorching down the table leaving paw prints in mustard as he ran, and streaked over Ninian's shoulder as if it were a mere fence, hotly pursued by Jingo, who did the same. Ninian jumped up in a passion and left the room without finishing his meal. With the strange equanimity of despair Violet saw him drive away in the Rolls.

Sir Alfred arrived punctually at the hour he had suggested, and surprised her. In Billy's descriptions he figured as barely human, whereas he proved to be a gentle, melancholy creature with a strong family likeness to Billy himself. He greeted Violet with simple friendliness, apologized for having to be a nuisance and apparently looked on the monkey's abduction as a capital joke.

"I am so relieved to find you taking it like this," Violet said. "You did sound rather vexed on the telephone, you know!"

"That wasn't I," Sir Alfred told her. "That was my secretary, Miss Nightingale."

"It was a man's voice, I thought," Violet said doubtfully.

"She used to be in the Army," replied Sir Alfred, and something of Billy's haunted look crept into his large, thoughtful eyes.

"Oh." Violet was a little nonplussed. "And so you have forgiven dear Billy."

"Yes," Sir Alfred said. "I see his point. He doesn't see mine. He should be mum-mum-mum mum-mum-mum . . . ade to walk round a children's hospital every day."

Violet's expectation of the trouble in store was gravely short of what indeed took place. Olimpia did not so much feel and express a grief as suddenly turn into very Grief itself. She stood before them in her white apron, her classical features convulsed, embodying all the pain, the loss, the transience of the world and at the same time managing in the wonderful Latin way to enjoy herself famously. Beautiful Italian phrases galloped from her lips and fell over each other as they came, while Tito, his face aglow with unbounded sympathy and limitless pride, translated here and there for Sir Alfred's sake.

"She say, now has nothing for her to life. She better dead."

"She say, better cut out the heart from the, the . . . petto," Tito thumped his own breast here, "than Desdemona. She better life wizzout heart than wizzout Desdemona."

"She say, il Signore Manley never use her come Lei. Is gentleman."

These last words fell on Violet's ear like the toll of a funeral bell.

What added to the poignancy of the scene was the conduct of little Desdemona herself. She flew to the arms of her intending murderer with cries of joy and perched on his shoulder, grinning delightedly and clapping her tiny hands: at which Olimpia broke down and sobbed as if her heart would break, while Tito threw out his arms with a grimace of scorn. "Il femminile!" he groaned. Sir Alfred was appalled by the effect his mission was having. With English delicacy he refrained until the very last from making the one point that the Riccis would understand: namely, that monkeys cost money. The work at the Oxford Foundation was carried on with funds provided by some very generous American called (Sir Alfred believed) Carnegie, and he did not feel at liberty to fritter away those funds on monkeys for all. When at last he could bring himself to broach the subject there was a marvellous transformation. While Olimpia clasped her hands and with the tears still running down her face launched into a hymn of thanksgiving and praise, Tito tore from the room, to return clasping an old tin chest stuffed with notes and coin. Both now prepared themselves for a long and splendid haggle; but another oldfangled English idea Sir Alfred had was that servants must never pay for things. Smiling, he told them that since she meant so much Desdemona was to remain and that the price of her should come from his pocket: a pocket, had he known it, lighter than theirs, for as well as their combined fantastic wages they obtained, from the Silverwood fruit and flowers, an income tidy even after McCardle had taken his cut.

These words produced a very tumult and it was some little time before Sir Alfred could hear himself speak. At last the Italians went away, fresh as flowers in the morning, leaving the English limp with emotion. Desdemona looked back in sorrow at Sir Alfred as Olimpia triumphantly bore her from the room and drew her breath with a sobbing cough.

"You are most kind," Violet said, touched. "But I think you must let me pay for the monkey. It is very well worth it, I can tell you."

Sir Alfred believed too that ladies should never pay for anything. "I couldn't allow it," he said, "but I will ask you to bring your influence to bear on William. He thinks the world of you both, and these episodes are becoming rather awkward. Everyone at the Foundation knows who is responsible. Now, I intensely dislike the music of today, which William loves: what would he say if I kidnapped his drummer or a flautist to try and prevent a performance? There must, if society is to function, be a certain give-and-take in these mum-mum-mum . . . atters."

"I think you may put your mind at rest," Violet assured him. "My brother spoke very seriously after the last time and Billy gave his word that it should not happen again."

Sir Alfred looked at her with a smile.

Mist was rising, Violet noted as she stood for a moment on the steps after seeing Sir Alfred off: one of those autumn mists that came creeping over the ground from the river and swallowed everything up.

Already the great copper beech had vanished into its maw and a long clammy tremulous arm was feeling a way towards the house. She turned to go, but heard the sound of an approaching motor and waited, her heart in her mouth, supposing that Ninian was back from court; but it was only a van, with the headlights burning. It drew up at the foot of the steps and the driver leaned out of his window waving a dispatch book.

"Sign, please," he called out, without leaving his seat.

"For what?" asked Violet, annoyed.

"Seven sheep," the man replied.

"There must be a mistake," Violet said. "Nobody here has ordered sheep." But the apprehension in her voice belied the words.

"This is Silverwood Court, isn't it?" the man said impatiently. "Have a heart, lady, the fog round here is cruel and I've got to get back to Abingdon. These sheep are for Silverwood Court. There's a gentleman with them," he added, as if he had just remembered it.

A vigorous thumping was now heard from the interior of the van. Mystified, Violet walked down the steps and turned the handle, whereupon the doors flew open and in the dim, richly scented interior she could just make out the pale woolly forms of the animals and the recumbent one of a gasping man.

"Huh-huh-huh hullo," said Billy. He got painfully out of the vehicle and stood before her, breathing hard and picking the wool from his clothes.

"Now what is the meaning of this?" she asked severely. "It is really too bad. Your brother has just been here. We are having trouble enough, Billy. And I think you gave Ninian your word."

"What is a pup-pup promise," Billy demanded with emotion, "compared to mum-mum-mum mum-mum-mum . . . otherhood?" He fished out of his pocket and handed to her a written statement which he had prepared beforehand, knowing that, spoken, it would take too long. It said: "These innocent ewes are the victims of a diabolical plot, which I only discovered by a happy chance. They are pregnant, and my wicked brother means to inject them experimentally, to see if the injection causes them to abort. What useful purpose can be served by this? And even were there one, how could it justify the cruel depriving of these, God's creatures, of the deepest, most beautiful, experience in life? Stand by them, Ninian/Violet, if your heart be flesh and not of stone: receive and protect them and thwart my brother of his fiendish purpose." A thought struck him and, taking the paper from her hand again, he crossed out the word Ninian and gave the document back.

"Billy, I do believe you will have to be certified," Violet said.

"Are you going to sign?" the driver shouted from his cabin. "I haven't got all day."

"Most certainly not," Violet said. "You will have to take these animals back whence they came."

These words resulted in the man's springing from his seat and running round to the back. "Coo, cripes, lady, have a heart," he remonstrated. "A nice way my van's going to be in."

"You'll be in a nicer one still, if you are not careful," Violet answered. "These sheep are stolen."

"V-V-V . . . iolet! . . . iolet!"

"Stolen?" ejaculated the driver. He pointed a truculent finger at the despairing Billy. "This cove said they was refugees."

"Stolen," Violet repeated grimly.

As if aware that her future was fraught with hazard, the ewe nearest the door now rose to her feet and jumped from the van, followed in sheepish discipline by all the others. Bleating, they stumbled away into the fog with Violet and Billy hastening after them, while the man hurriedly got into the machine again and drove off as quickly as he dared. The animals took the direction of the flower gardens, innocently trampling over beds, fouling immaculate paths and knocking down the few remaining blooms of McCardle's show chrysanthemums.

"Try and head them off, Billy," Violet panted. "If we can get them round to the front they perhaps will settle down on the lawn."

Billy's valiant attempt to comply with her wish merely diverted them towards one of the greenhouses, from which McCardle was coming out with a basket of grapes. The gardener halted abruptly and glared at them from under his bushy sandy brows. "What's a-gaein' on the noo?" he demanded in a threatening tone of voice, while the ewes grouped themselves about him and bleated in chorus.

"These are sheep, McCardle," Violet stated.

"Sheep, forbye!" snarled the gardener. "Do ye not ken a yoe in lamb when you see her?"

"Be that as it may," Violet said. "I am afraid they will have to spend the night here."

McCardle took off his cap and flung it to the

ground. "Over ma daid body, then," he retorted. Well-nigh incomprehensible speech flowed steadily from his lips from which his listeners gathered that never since the beginning of time was a man more badgered, tormented, put upon and underprized than himself; and the revolution was a long time in coming. But as he spoke a strange difference became apparent in him. His Border Scottish blood began to work, ancestral memories awoke, they grew, they caught fire, and with the ewes rubbing about his legs and nibbling his grapes, bit by bit McCardle's face took on a jovial aspect that made it difficult to recognize. He continued cursing and grumbling, to be sure, but with his cheeks now split in a happy grin. "I'll no bide here, to be dreven like the heathen black," he said, beaming. "There's aye some new outrage in this place," he chortled. "I canna have flower nor fruit, stalk nor stem, but some mischeevious beastie comes traidin' it underfoot," he said, looking fondly down at them: and they, knowing their friend, looked up and all bleated together again. "Nay, then, ma beauties, come away, come away," he said softly and tenderly and, with a final look of loathing for Miss La Touche, set off for the stables with the ewes trotting in perfect confidence at his heels.

"Well, that is that for the moment," Violet said. One extra problem was hardly noticeable these days. "Come to the house, Billy. I must see if Ninian is back."

"He is rather gug-gug going it, isn't he?" Billy remarked as they walked up the path together. Violet sighed.

There was no sign of her brother or the Rolls, no telephoned message as to the result of the case, and the mist grew denser all the time. Violet lingered awhile at the open door, shivering, in case there should come the sound of an engine. "He will never get back in all this," she said presently, shutting the door and leading Billy to the library. "What an evening," she said almost in anger, as she picked up the telephone. "Why, the mist has even got into the house: one cannot see the books on the shelves."

Billy looked round the brilliantly lighted room in surprise, and at Violet herself. Then with a cry he ran forward to help her as she slipped, fainting, to the floor.

"Miss La Touche, Miss La Touche," said Dr Benn, when his examination was ended. "What shall I do with you? You really must try and relax."

"Relax!" she groaned. "With all the things I must see to!"

"Are these 'things' really worth it?" he demanded with his piercing look.

"Oh, Doctor! If women start asking themselves that . . . !" They smiled at each other; and in the next moment the door opened and Ninian stood there.

"Well well well, here is our juvenile delinquent," Dr Benn remarked. "What is it to be? Borstal or the birch? Don't tell me you're growing a beard. I forbid it absolutely. A beard is a food trap at any time, but for a man of your beastly habits it is not to be thought of. It will be all glued together like one of those birds' nests the Chinese put into soup."

"Witty as ever, I notice," Ninian said in great good humour, and to Violet: "Five pounds and a scolding. A mere bagatelle. And they never saw me driving away."

"Thank God," Violet said, lying back on the sofa.

"I fear you are becoming a little blasé," Dr Benn proceeded. "And I had so hoped it would be the birch! Well, I must leave you or Mrs Benn will imagine that I have gone to the dogs as well." As Ninian escorted him through the hall, "Look after her, La Touche," he said sternly. "You are worrying her into her . . . you are wearing her out with all your nonsense. Stop it. We none of us last forever, you know."

Ninian turned a little pale. "Violet is made of steel, really she is," he assured the frowning Dr. Benn. "Women are always fainting. It is not as if I were to faint. But as a matter of fact, I feel none too well. I don't go in for fussing about my health, but I would be glad if you could give me a look-over sometime soon. You haven't a few moments to spare just now?"

"No," Dr Benn agreed. "I have not." He shook hands and trotted down the steps to his jeep, vaulting over the side with a little cry of pain. "Shocking pity it wasn't the birch," he called out, and drove valiantly into the deepening fog.

Thirteen

Now the blow fell at last: the Riccis gave notice that early in the New Year they would enter the service of Mr John Manley, historian. On Manley's side were the Italian villa and the amazing knowledge of Italy, as well as the fact that Tito had been compelled to wait on Mr Piper; and after impassioned debates that often lasted till cockcrow the pair had agreed to forego the greater comfort and higher wages of Silverwood and its various emoluments. They imagined that when they were in his employ Manley still would regale them with spicy historical gossip about their birthplaces, still quote Dante to them, still discuss with Tito, as man to man, the Italian politics of the day. He had warmly consented to Desdemona making her home with them, while secretly he planned to have her murdered. No argument had any effect on them, although they said that separation from Violet and Ninian would undoubtedly break their hearts.

After five years of the Ricci warmth, cleverness and prodigious hard work, the La Touches hardly knew how they should manage without them. They could not conceive that a relationship, meaning so much to them and apparently to the Riccis too, could come thus lightly to an end with the formal month's notice; and it helped to bring home in a cruel way what was already in the minds of both, namely, the impermanence of earthly things and the fleeting nature of peace and contentment.

"We must try and look on the bright side," Ninian said. The disaster brought him and Violet closer together than they had been for some time.

"There is none," she replied. "Except that Manley will hardly come here once he has them."

"For all their qualities, I suspect they were not entirely honest," he went on. "I have an idea they helped themselves to things in the hothouses."

"Oh, Ninian, as if it mattered!" Violet looked at him in wonder. "Figs and grapes and peaches are so plentiful in Italy. They can have had no idea of their value."

"Quite true," he said. "I'm talking nonsense."

After a triumph like this anyone else might have had the grace to lie low and take things quietly. Manley trumpeted his success to the four winds: he boasted everywhere of his tactics, jeered at the La Touches' defeat, expatiated on the meals he meant to enjoy and even laughed at the Riccis for their simple trust. The victory drove even the impending publication of the *magnum opus* from his mind and revealed to him a hidden strain of mysticism in his nature.

"It all seems in a mysterious way to have been intended," he confided to a colleague at Oxford. "I am not a religious man, McCarthy, but when I think of that woman's food . . ." He broke off, overcome.

On the other hand, "If there were such a being as God," Ninian said with solemnity, "He would surely intervene."

The rapprochement of brother and sister lasted only a short time. Violet was near the end of patience and Ninian seemed all at once to enjoy tormenting her. He was wholly unpredictable these days, no one knew what he would say or do next except that all his former opinions and tastes were now rejected with scorn. He read the works of Mr Novak again and again and discussed them tirelessly at mealtimes until Violet was all but unconscious with boredom. Nevertheless, the more erratic he grew himself the more affronted he was by erratic behaviour in others: he could not bear anyone else to be strange for a moment.

"What's all that? What's the man about?" he exploded, staring out of the drawing-room window one sunny afternoon.

Violet told him that McCardle was erecting a fold for the ewes on the lawn, where the grass was softer and richer than in the meadows.

"On my lawn? I won't have it." He had acquired

a habit of talking to her in these machine-gun bursts. "And those sheep. Why are they still here?"

"If they go, McCardle goes."

"We have been slaves of McCardle long enough." For a time he grumbled and growled to himself, like an elderly dog. "It is stealing, Violet. Billy is a thief. And he broke his word. I will never speak to him again."

In the past the La Touches had often smiled together over Billy's shady little ways, which, in truth, had endeared him to them almost as much as his gentle humanity.

"And I am responsible!" Ninian cried with intense bitterness. "A century ago I would have been hanged."

"You may yet be, as it is."

They were none the better pleased with each other for this little brush, and far worse was to come with Ninian's disclosure of his latest plan. He had decided to go at once to Barcelona and Madrid to get in touch with various abstract painters now coming up and to go on afterwards to La Cabeza, a simple fishing village on the Costa del Sol that he had loved as a boy. At present he had an overpowering urge to see and hear again the sights and sounds of his youth; and he was taking Mercy with him. To Violet, however, he spoke merely of Barcelona and Madrid and abstract painters.

"But are you not running things rather fine?" she asked. "Christmas will be on before we know it."

"My dear girl. I shan't be here for Christmas."

"Not here!" Violet looked at him in bewilderment. Their Christmas followed a routine laid down many years ago and, although they pooh-pooh'd it, it was a time of happiness for them both. Well in advance they sent out their cards, of original design and in perfect taste, and chuckled over the horrors that came pouring in. They groaned at all the neighbours' invitations, and had genuine pleasure in accepting them. They gave a party for the village children and a dance for the young people, there were presents for the old and impoverished, former servants and tenants were called on one by one on Christmas Eve, and Christmas trees decorated and hung with gifts were sent to the hospital. All these things took careful thought and a lot of hard work, of which the lion's share always fell to Violet: she had begun her preparations sometime before and had been intending to discuss them with her brother when the Riccis' thunderbolt drove all else into the background. And he sat there, coolly declaring that he would be away!

"No," he said. "I cannot bear the idea of all those stuffy county jollifications."

"Do not allow that to put you off," Violet replied. "This year we are not invited to any."

"What!" Ninian jumped up and went across to the table where invitation cards were always set out. "How vindictive, how mean!" he exclaimed, having verified her statement. "We should never have gone to them at all. It was a great mistake to mix with the landed savagery. But that's neither here nor there. I must go away. I am tired of always doing the same things over and over again."

"So are we all," Violet replied. "But the people will expect to see you."

"Then I must disappoint them."

"Isolowolotumba arrives on Boxing Day: you invited him yourself," Violet persisted. "If you are not here he is bound to assume it is because he is black."

"I cannot help what he is bound to assume."

"Then I will shut the house and go away myself," Violet cried in sudden anger. "I cannot do it all alone."

"But what about the parties? We have always given them," Ninian said reproachfully. "And poor Isolowolotumba? It is not like you to be selfish."

"Why must you go now? Why not wait until the Riccis leave? Then we can both go away, forever if we like."

"Things cannot wait, in the art world," Ninian said with importance.

"And Miss Fellowe goes with you, I presume."

"I do not altogether see the relevance," Ninian replied pompously. "And in any case I have not yet decided about it."

The three Siamese cats were at luncheon again that day, a thing Violet had never allowed before when Miss Fellowe was in the house. She fed them all copiously from her plate while her brother winced and nagged, paying no heed to him whatever and presently going so far as to take a piece of chicken from her mouth and give it to Pibun. Muttering under his breath, Ninian rose and left the room.

"Sometimes I think my brother is not as fond of cats as I," Violet said to Mercy. She spoke quite pleasantly, for she had never been able to dislike the child very much after seeing her run to save Mary's pictures.

"He says they are possessed by demons," Mercy said timidly. She both enjoyed and was frightened by the mounting tension in the household, believing herself to be the sole cause of it.

"Really?" Violet smiled at Miss Fellowe for the first time since she had come to the house. "He knows more about that than I." She continued, as far as the requirements of Taikun, Jingo and Pibun would allow, to pass amiable remarks now and then for the rest of the meal.

Is she, Mercy later breathed at her looking glass, trying to come between us?

Ninian paced up and down in his study, thoughtfully stroking his beard and thinking that the sooner he and Mercy went away the better. The gloves were truly off when Violet no longer cared what Mercy saw and thought. It occurred to him that very likely the child had no passport and that, since she was under age, Mumsie would have to endorse her application for one. The further horrid idea struck him that Mumsie's consent would have to be obtained before he took her abroad at all. 'Must be prepared to travel' had been, with first-class shorthand and typing and previous experience of similar work, a desideratum in his advertisement; but what if she, or Mumsie, made as light of that one as of all the others? He had quite set his heart on having her all to himself for a while in a foreign country, away from familiar things and places: why, he hardly knew. He could not have said what he expected or hoped would come of it, he had no evil plans for a seduction, no ridiculous ones for a marriage. It was as if all the longing and wildness and half-sweet misery in his heart were boiling over and could be contained no more.

"Would you like to come with me to Madrid, kitten?" he asked when Mercy presented herself, twenty minutes' late, for the afternoon's work. They continued to observe this ritual, although there was little or nothing for them to do. Since the day of the private viewing the gallery had given no sign of life at all. Reynolds referred nothing to Ninian, neither the points arising from the Taplin show, a great success despite its unhappy beginning, nor those connected with the Isolowolotumba one with which London was to be startled in May. Such conduct in his very junior partner struck Ninian as outrageous, on a par with that of Violet and the Siamese cats and Mary's mischievous prank at the *vernissage*. He felt that he was surrounded by people who had flung all discipline and decorum to the winds and who fastened on his own external acts to justify themselves, unaware of how very different his case was; and yet, lazy as a man in fever, he could not rouse himself to deal with them.

"Oh, Ninny!" Mercy had a confused vision of orange trees, guitars, bulls and a girl named Conchita González who had been in her typing class at the Polytechnic. "Oh, yes, Ninny!"

"You will have to get leave from your mother," he said. "She may think you a little too young."

"Oh, Mumsie lets me do as I like," Mercy assured

him. "Specially if it's you. She said when you got the chairs and tables back that she'd go through hell and high water for you."

"Let us hope that it won't be necessary," he said. "But will you mind being away for Christmas?"

"Oh, no," Mercy cried with emphasis. "Dad always turns up then and they shout and quarrel and throw things. Then when at last he goes away Mumsie cries and drinks cherry brandy and says she would like to be dead. I can't bear Christmas!" She was about to go on but caught herself up, and a flush that began somewhere far away out of sight crept slowly over her neck and face.

"I see," Ninian said, after a pause. He did see: he was beginning to see a good deal, but it made no difference at all.

Mercy had a passport because Eva Bernstein had been going to take her to Ostende for a week the summer before, only it fell through at the last moment. She'd been terribly upset at the time, but just think, if she had gone she would never have seen Ninian's advertisement! "Fate willed it otherwise," she said, looking uncomfortably like her mother.

"Shall I need tropical clothes for Madrid, Ninny?" she asked anxiously then, entirely recovered from the embarrassment of a few moments ago, her great eyes helplessly at odds with each other in the way he loved.

"Not in December, my pet. More likely a thick fur coat, Russian boots and a piece of blubber to suck," he told her.

"I haven't got those either," she said with a sigh.

"We'll do a little shopping in London." And with

these words, he knew, the point of no return was left behind.

Mrs Fellowe was very far from objecting to the journey proposed, although she insisted on coming to Silverwood to talk it over. She had long pined to see the house and grounds and it was something of a grievance that Ninian had never invited her there; but hitherto she had considered that too much was at stake for her to yield to natural impulse and simply push in. Now she had a pretext: two pretexts in fact, for Mercy had confessed to the appalling slip she had made concerning her father.

"Don't think the worse of her, Ninian, for a harmless little fib or so," she pleaded, goggling at him from under her close-fitting pink feather hat. She had plunged into the subject as soon as she had fussily sat down, first smoothing her coat behind to avoid creasing. "The hubby and I are estranged, and she minds about it. That's why she says I'm a widow."

"Please, please," Ninian began but she swept on.

"I've done nothing to be ashamed of, I'm sure," she declared. "That hand"—she held out a grimy palm for him to look at—"is clean. But I married beneath me, let's face it. And Mercy minds him being a traveller."

"Mrs Fellowe, please," Ninian tried again.

"Olga!" she cried.

"I have no wish at all to pry into your family matters," he said. "I want to know if you have any objection to Mercy coming abroad with me."

"She's her own mistress," Mumsie replied, adding with a leer, "least, I don't know that she's anyone else's so far." She chuckled over this sally for a while.

"I suppose," she remarked, borne forward on the wings of her own wit, "I ought to say, young man, what are your intentions?" And now she laughed long and loud, wafting the fragrance of stale tobacco on the air.

Ninian listened to her with feelings akin to those called up by the comic postcard. "I am going to Madrid on business," he said coldly. "I always take a secretary when I travel. Mercy is younger than the other women I have employed, and so I have consulted you."

Mrs Fellowe gave him the shrewd self-satisfied look of a thoroughly stupid woman. "Be your age, now do," she said, chuckling again. "Is it a typist's job to say if the boss shall grow a beard? All right, all right! But I'm Mercy's mother, when all is said and done. And a girl's good name," she declaimed, with a resurgence of the histrionic, "is her all!"

"Hers is in no danger from me." Ninian felt really weak with disgust and humiliation to feel that his happiness lay in the power of this creature. "And if I may say so, I have my own reputation to think about."

"Hoity-toity! Come off it, you naughty boy!" The gooseberry jellies gleamed in merciless recollection. Ninian became aware of the hostility under the badinage and put it down to motherly concern for the child. In fact, it arose from the arrangement he had made about her tables and chairs. These had been redelivered to the teashop as soon as he could see to it, and Mumsie had lived in hourly expectation of a visit from him at which, patting her hand, he was to have said, "And now, little lady, what other debts have we?" She even confided to cronies that she knew for sure, although they mustn't ask her how, that this visit would come off; but nothing happened, and it was rankling sorely. "Reputation, indeed! You men are all the same." And indeed in her presence Ninian did feel strangely reduced to some crude common level of masculinity, much like a man in a brothel.

He made a new attempt to dispose of her. "I put in my advertisement that applicants for the post here must be ready to travel," he said, panting a little as if the interview were overtaxing him. "But if you have any objection, there is no more to be said. I understood you had none." He thought suddenly, with a shiver, that she might propose to come with them.

"I am a mother, Ninian!" Mumsie cried, flinging wide her arms. "I want everything for my little girl that life can offer—travel, books, music, culture, furs. But whatever should I do," now she spoke in a hoarse undertone, "if one day my little girl should come to me and say, 'Mumsie, there are going to be three of us!'"

"Please, Mrs Fellowe, please!" he besought her in agony, thinking his cup must surely now be full.

"You'll tell me you're past it," she swept on with a judicial air, restraining him, by a movement of the hand, from putting this argument forward. "Ah, but I've known stranger things at sea. Things you'd hardly credit," she said, and the gleam of recollection reappeared. "And so how do I know but what my little girlie's going to be had for a mug?" And leaning back in her chair she surveyed him with the complacence of a woman who knows she is handling a delicate matter well.

185

"It will be best, I think," he said exhaustedly, "if Mercy stays at home." But he knew that she would not stay at home.

"No, no! Not that!" Mumsie cried in terror. "She would never forgive me. Her heart is set on going. She doesn't even know that her old Mumsie is talking to you like this."

"What, then, do you want?"

"My little girl's happiness!" Mumsie exclaimed, vigorously throwing her arms out again as if trying to keep fit. What she wanted really was an enjoyable scene, followed by a peep at the rooms upstairs.

"And so do I," he assured her. "After all, if I had any of the base intentions you ascribe to me I need not carry the child off abroad. What should stop me trying to seduce her here?"

Mumsie discarded her dramatic line in favour of the coy and confidential. "So you've been thinking about it!" she laughed, turning her head away the better to slide him a roguish glance.

The grain of truth in this remark was past enduring. Ninian abruptly rose to his feet and said that she would have to excuse him, as he had much to attend to before he left. The action distressed his visitor beyond words: she had forked out ten bob for someone to mind the café and was wearing her feather hat and good black coat on the supposition that she would be invited, pressed, commanded to stay to luncheon at least. Her dream relationship with Ninian had developed apace and by now she saw herself as firmly rooted in his affections, so that all this sudden strange aloofness pierced her to the heart.

"Must I go, then?" she asked wistfully. "I have never yet broken bread under your roof, Ninian." It sounded as if she had enjoyed all manner of other experiences there. "And I did so want to see Viola's bedroom! Mercy has told me so much about it, that white and gold and all."

"I didn't realize she had ever been inside," he said with disdain.

"Oh, Mercy doesn't miss much." Sighing, Mumsie got to her feet. "You're not going my way? There isn't a bus for ages."

"Tito will call a taxi for you," he said, leading the way to the door at something like a sprint. "I am not allowed to drive."

"Oh, of course! You naughty sporty boy!" But the old brio was gone. "Little Olga can't afford taxis," she resumed with pathos.

"We have an account with this man." He could bear no more and took to his heels, shouting for Tito as if the house were on fire. While the Italian telephoned for the taxi he took refuge in the men's downstair cloakroom, actually concealing himself behind the garments hanging on the wall, half-expecting Mumsie to come burrowing through them after him like an excited terrier. "Bloody bloody bloody woman!" he snarled through grinding teeth. Every encounter with her was fraught with horror, not merely in itself but for the devastating illumination it spread all round. The fact that Mercy had been vulgar enough to go prying about Violet's bedroom was bad enough; but it also seemed to put a new complexion on matters that once had amused or touched him, such as her confidence in applying for the job at all and her audacity in drawing Mrs Bentley on the study wall. And still, hapless wight, he counted the minutes until he should find himself alone with her, abroad.

After what seemed a very long time he heard the taxi arrive and, after more time, drive off. He left his hiding place and wearily walked across the hall to the library, thinking that a little Bach before luncheon might give him back his peace of mind. To his fury, the shining walnut sides of the radio-Gram were newly scarred by the claws of the Siamese; and as he went to get a record he saw the body of a mouse finally, mercifully, dead after hours of their play. All at once he felt he was going mad. He flew to the bell and kept his finger on it until Tito came running in with alarm in his face. He was quite unable to speak but, shaking all over, his face the colour of parchment, simply pointed to the little corpse on the floor.

"What is it? What is it?" cried Olimpia, breathless with anticipation as Tito came back with the mouse delicately rolled up in a sheet of paper.

Greatly enjoying himself, Tito slowly undid the paper and with a dramatic flourish held out the defunct mouse on his open palm for her to see. Next he shrugged his shoulders until they rose well above his ears. Then with his left forefinger he slowly described a loop in the air beside his left temple.

"Mamma mia!" Olimpia gasped and gave herself up wholeheartedly to a long, joyous, silvery peal of laughter, while from her downy cot beside the ovens little Desdemona shrieked and shook hands with herself above her head like a triumphant pugilist.

Fourteen

"This always seems like a miracle," Ninian said. The aeroplane had shot up through the wet grey cloud that darkened London and was flying southward in a mighty dome of blue and gold, with that same cloud lying far below in a fiery feathery sea. "Our soft, dark, introversive weather has helped produce one of the finest literatures in the world, and some comfortable furniture. But how good to be reminded of what lies above and beyond!"

He was trying to take Miss Fellowe's mind off the fear that had suddenly overwhelmed it as the aeroplane rose. Until that moment all her thoughts had been of abroad and Ninian and the fine new clothes she was wearing, that made her look so wonderfully much older. So enchanted was she with her red coat and its astrakhan collar that she refused to take it off, although the socket above her head was belching hot air with all its might. It was only as the great vessel roared and shook, collecting its powers for the mad rush over the tarmac before it hurled itself into space, that she knew she was afraid: as it swayed and rattled and dropped into air pockets on the way up she all but melted with terror; and when the notice about smoking and safety belts was switched off, she leaped to the conclusion that the engines had failed and lay back in her seat with eyes closed, as white as paper. Why, why had she ever come? Something told her that this day was to be her last.

Ninian went on talking but she seemed not to hear. He told her that all round the globe hundreds and thousands of other people were in the air that very minute, that this was the mode of travel of our day, that once upon a time people had been just as frightened in trains, that one was safer in the sky than on the road; and that in under four hours they would be laughing about it together in Madrid. But fear had hooked itself on to her mind like a bat, and at last, having never suffered from this form of it, he grew a little impatient. No backbone in this genera-tion, he thought, meaning Miss Fellowe and Mr Pi-per.

"Come now, my dear," he said gently, "this is not quite worthy of you."

"You've had your life," Mercy roused herself to moan.

It was not an auspicious beginning. Presently, as if worn out by the sheer force of her panic, she dozed off and leaning across her he looked out the window. After Bordeaux the cloud began to thin, giving brief glimpses of blue sea, a fringe of white spray picking out a coast line, a patchwork of tiny brown and green fields; and then again all cloud vanished entirely and, with poor Miss Fellowe muttering and moaning in her sleep, he saw far below the lovely ungainly tawny land of Castille.

Suddenly she woke with a start. "Why are you looking out of the window?" she exclaimed. "Oh, Ninny! Oh! The propellers have stopped!"

"My poor child, they are going so fast you cannot see them. Don't you see that curious thing like a ball of fire whirling in front of each engine?"

"Fire!" She slumped in her seat, bereft of even the strength to feel afraid.

He laughed and took her cold shivering little hand in his. "Courage! We are nearly there. That dark patch spilled out over the ground is Avila. Now hold on to your hat. Very soon we shall be going down."

When they left the aeroplane it was Ninian's turn to be alarmed, as the weather was sharper than he had expected and the word pneumonia! flashed across his brain like a road warning. "I think we must stay in the hotel this evening," he said, apprehensively turning up the collar of his coat. "Nothing is more dangerous than a sudden drop in temperature. And in Madrid there is a wicked little wind that creeps down from the snowy Sierras and lies in waiting round the corner. There are hundreds of deaths every year."

"Oh, don't let us be fussy." Mercy knew she had been foolish and now was thoroughly cross, while the bewildering experience of being in a foreign country among strange people, understanding nothing of what they said or did, made her want to criticize and disparage. "I think Spaniards are very inefficient," was her verdict when they had waited a quarter of an hour for their luggage.

"I didn't know you made a fetish of competence," he mocked at her.

"They wouldn't do this at London."

"The last time I went through London airport they sent my baggage to Zürich instead of Amsterdam. Their famous electronic brain had evidently been in the bar. Dear child," he begged her, "don't begin finding fault with everything Spaniards do. It is so terribly provincial."

"I am proud to be English," she said with dignity.

Her Englishness grew more and more pronounced as the evening wore on. She had "never heard of anything so ridiculous" as dinner at half-past ten and after eating the excellent French meal the hotel provided didn't "think much of Spanish food." Ninian became exasperated. He was suffering in his mind from the amused, politely knowing attitude of the hotel staff, who had allotted them communicating bedrooms without being asked to and who referred to the obviously immature Mercy with ironic courtesy as "la Señora." They had pigeonholed him in one of the half-dozen human situations they recognized, effectively demoting him in much the way that Mumsie did and with the same hideous grain of justification.

"I think we had better go to bed," he said. "To-morrow we have things to attend to."

Tomorrow came and no business was done. Both of them had slept well and were in good spirits, and Ninian thought that Mercy should see something of the capital before they began their work. In the morning he took her to the Prado, putting it to himself, but without any fervent conviction, that the more she looked at painting the greater her usefulness as his secretary would become. Mercy trotted after him through the long galleries with unconcealed indifference. She saw no further use in culture now, and would have greatly preferred to look at the shops; and she appalled him by an entirely new habit of saying "Gosh!" in full reply to his interesting remarks.

"We've improved our minds enough for one day," he said at luncheon. "What would you like to do this evening? Madrid dozes now until round about five."

"I should like to go to a bullfight," she replied without hesitation. So far she had seen nothing at all like the leaflets in the travel agency.

"I am afraid there are none before Easter. The bulls are a summer-time affair."

"But I read in some paper that Spaniards all go to football matches now instead. Don't tell me," Mercy exclaimed, looking thoroughly English at once, "that they play football in the summer too!"

Ninian smiled. "No, that is just a myth," he said. "There will always be corridas while there is a Spain."

"Do you like them, Ninny? Mumsie says they're just a lot of nasty cruel foreigners showing off."

"They are too much for me," he admitted. "My fibres are not strong. But there is great beauty, grace

193

and skill in a good one. But I think what moves the Spaniard is the resolution and courage and defiance. Death has a peculiar horror for people as passionate and alive as they are, and to see a man frivolously hazard his life in the ring carries them away."

"Gosh!"

Since he could not provide a bullfight, Ninian thought he would take her to an evening of *flamenco*. There was a new dancer now appearing for the first time in Madrid after taking the Spanish Americas by storm, whom people spoke of as a new Pastora Imperio. Men were said to be going out of their minds for love of her, and the customary tales, circulated as a rule by the dancer's agent, of diamonds, rubies, emeralds showered upon her, of crazy routs and orgies offered by millionaires, of duels, were believed for once to contain some truth. And the curtain was not up on La Niña del Rosario for twenty seconds, she had not so much as moved a foot or clacked a castanet, before he knew that here was someone remarkable indeed. She moved to the music as if she and her guitarist had but one mind: she had a balance between abandon and control, passion and dignity, a fire and ice opposed, yet fusing in a whole that was both tragic and triumphant, that Ninian had but rarely seen before; and as the curtain fell and the wild shouts of admiration broke out all over the theatre he had tears in his eyes.

"What a noisy audience!" Mercy exclaimed, looking about with disapproval and lazily clapping her hands. "What was she doing?"

Ninian did his best to explain, wondering how on

194

earth anyone, even a little provincial nordic goose, could not know what La Niña had been doing.

"Gosh!" Then, as if herself aware that her responses fell a little short, she inquired with feigned interest, "But why dance to a banjo? Can't she afford a proper band?"

"That is a guitar," he said with the cadence of exhaustion. Away from Silverwood, with no one either attacking the girl or deriding his enslavement to her, he seemed to be listening to her prattle with a fresh ear. Ruefully he asked himself what had become of the various delightful qualities he once had found in it. It was as if in this land of harsh light and merciless clarity the soft balmy hazes of England were driven from the mind itself. Had he been but inventing talents for this child as a screen for a different kind of interest altogether, one that he could not bear to acknowledge?

"I think flamenco is a lot of fuss about nothing," came the verdict in her bright, common little voice at the evening's end.

"Do you indeed, little silly."

She tossed her head at the epithet, thinking it strange that her opinions were no longer received with the rapture and excitement of yore. Nothing was ever heard of her underlying lucidity these days. Can it be, she breathed into the huge Isabelline looking glass in her room before climbing into her vast creaking bed that night, that he is beginning to take me for granted? Sitting on her own little bed at home the night before she left, Mumsie had earnestly counselled her not to allow this to happen. But how did one prevent it? Her last thought before she fell asleep was to wonder why Mr La Touche made no pass at her. She would reject it, on Mumsie's advice again, but she had assumed it would be made. Mr Eccles, the organist at the Cathedral, had made a pass the second time they met; and he was a married man with four children as well as an organist.

Ninian lay awake until the dawn, his mind tormented by disagreeable thoughts and painful memories. He looked back to the Madrid he had known as a boy of fifteen, gaslit, romantic, stylish as a republican capital can seldom be: the short-legged, stern-faced officers in their absurdly wonderful uniforms, the carriages drawn by racy, high-stepping Andalusian horses, the leafy flowery parks, the glittering hissing fountains, the lights. He too had been taken to a performance of *flamenco* on his first evening in the city, nothing, he now supposed, comparable to what they had seen that night. He had been utterly swept off his feet and could only stammer foolishly when his father's host asked him how he liked it. He remembered those old Spanish friends, now dead every one, as they had sat in the box at the theatre, with their heavy dark faces, their moustaches and side whiskers, wearing the ornate continental evening dress and diamond rings on their little fingers, laughing at his emotion yet pleased and touched by it as well. How could anyone sit entirely unmoved through all that force and passion and life? What were these young people of today, these stolid inaccessible little creatures, these Mercys, these Pipers? Ah, but to compare one's juniors unfavourably with oneself at a similar age was an infallible sign of approaching senility, he thought; but he continued to do so for a long time none the less, as he lay staring with hot eyes into the darkness over his head.

Of the three abstract painters with whom Ninian had hoped to discuss a possible exhibition, Moreno and Ménendez were in prison and Loyola had gone to the mountains to ski. The latter would return after Christmas, the former perhaps in twenty years. Ninian decided that they would go on to La Cabeza without delay, and try to get in touch with Loyola on the journey home: once out of the sunshine Madrid was positively arctic and he took his temperature several times during the day, expecting the symptoms of pneumonia from one hour to the next.

Mercy welcomed the prospect of sun and orange trees and Andalusian glamour, but refused on any account whatsoever to take the aeroplane to Gibraltar, as he had arranged. They must, she said, go by rail: she would not undergo such an ordeal again, no, not for all the tea in China.

"It will be sixteen hours at least," he said in exasperation, "and we shall have to change at Bobadilla. No one takes the train in this country."

"Bobadilla sounds nice."

"Bobadilla is a pointless, featureless railway junction where travellers in the south of Spain are liable to stick, like flies in a web. No," he said with decision, "it is not to be borne. We must go on to Málaga and then double back along the coast to La Cabeza. It means two journeys instead of one but at least we may escape with our lives."

"I want to change at Bobadilla," she declared, in the imperious tone of a spoiled beauty.

"Then you'll have to do it by yourself," he told her drily, and she said no more, but gave the little toss of her head that was becoming habitual.

In the various dispositions of their trip to La Cabeza Spain surpassed even her own glittering records. To begin with, the hotel booked them on the wrong train: Ninian had asked for tickets on the morning express but the concierge got them for the slow train of the afternoon, and cajole, bluster and threaten as he might Ninian could not persuade the guard to allow them on the express. He was furious with himself, because he ought to have remembered that everything in Spain must be checked and because he knew, too, that had he been alone or in suitable company the other passengers would all have taken up the cudgels for him and argued and shouted and browbeaten the guard until he gave in; but that as one more immoral foreigner, travelling with a mistress indecently young, he had to be plagued and obstructed in every way possible. Thus they were obliged to hang about Madrid for most of the day with nothing to do and an all-night journey ahead, while Mercy frequently complained that Bobadilla would be screened from view by darkness and that it was really too bad. They were too late, the fat unshaven clerk in the office said, opening one eye like a drowsy dog, to reserve seats for that afternoon and they had to fight for places like the hundreds of Spaniards fiercely milling about them.

"I thought nobody went by rail in Spain," Mercy jeered when at last they were settled, wedged in between two enormous ladies who first turned the heating up as high as it would go and then fanned themselves with vigour.

The train jerked slowly and suspiciously forward, grunting. Darkness fell and the orange-tinted electric light in the carriage was so dull that even if their arms had not been pinned to their sides by their expansive neighbours they could not have read by it. Thirty miles out of Madrid an obstruction on the line held the train up for three-quarters of an hour, so that it lost its place in the dazing hotchpotch of Spanish railroads and was continually shunted into sidings to allow some other train to pass, growing later and later itself and consequently having to give place to more and more other trains. Expecting to reach Málaga at six in the morning, they had brought no food; and Mercy had forgotten to pack the corkscrew for their bottle of wine.

"We may yet be there by noon," Ninian said with forced calm.

He knew how dangerous such forecasts are, for almost invariably a lurking Spanish demon feels itself challenged by them. A horrible, seemingly endless night followed, in which neither of them closed an eye. With the terrifying vitality and total unconcern for others of their race, the Spaniards talked loudly among themselves throughout, and screamed in unison when Ninian tried to open the window. Soon after ten, the train limped into Valdepeñas and men were heard shouting at each other as they ran up and down the track, dealing the train a series of heavy blows with iron bars that rang through Ninian's aching head as if itself were being struck. The man in the corner seat eagerly put his head out of the window and began shouting as well: then drew it in again with a satisfied air.

"There is a fault in the train," he reported proudly.

"Ay, Dios!" Ninian muttered.

The Spaniards looked at him with expressions ranging from disapproval to hatred.

"Such things happen in every country," the man in the corner said. "In Germany, England, France . . . Everywhere you will find little flaws of organization. Spain stands high in this respect."

"If foreigners do not like it here, they need not come."

"A foreigner should behave as a guest in another man's house."

They glowered at him and at Mercy and at him again. What can we expect from immoral Protestant strangers? their faces said.

Ninian painfully rose to his feet, intending to go and see what refreshments were to be had. As he climbed down the precipitous steps the railwaymen began shouting to him to get back at once as the train was about to leave. Resuming his seat, he waited for half an hour and then sallied forth again, accompanied this time by the man in the corner. While he argued with the woman in the buffet as to whether he might take cup and saucer to the compartment, the train set off at a lively pace and vanished whistling round the bend of a hill.

"It will return," said his companion, with the Spaniard's clairvoyance in such matters. He now threw himself heart and soul into the debate about the cup and saucer, on Ninian's side, and with entire success; and having thus wiped out the shame of the breakdown paid for all Ninian bought with immense good humour.

Ten minutes later the train came bowling into view once more, but on a different and subsidiary line.

"That is so other trains may proceed," said the man, with the air of a guide displaying a national treasure. "In other lands the line would be blocked for hours. Here we shall sit, until the fault is found and repaired. If not, when we come to the mountain pass . . ." He hurled himself to the ground and waved his boots in the air to communicate an idea of disaster, Ninian's excellent Spanish having failed to convince him that he could otherwise be understood.

They sat there, indeed, until twenty past four. Twice the train was cleared of all passengers, on the ground that an extra rapido luxury train was coming specially for their relief; and twice it proved to be an illusion. On returning to their compartment the second time Ninian found their two places occupied by Civil Guards, wooden-faced under their fanciful glossy hats, who apparently heard not a word of his appeals. There was nothing the weary pair could do but perch on some bundles they found in the corridor.

Spain did truly seem resolved that day to show off her inexhaustible powers of invention. She seemed, too, to find a diabolical glee in wrecking whatever it was he had, or thought he had, with Mercy Fellowe. Like a boxer pitilessly raining blows on a wilting enemy, she fired off one thing after another that caused them both to reveal themselves in a new, disturbing or irritating light. As the frightful day crept on, Mercy's Englishness, her pride in which had so often struck Ninian as inappropriate, began to manifest itself in a more attractive way. Exhausted and cramped and starving as she was, she now determined to make the best of things, she forbore to complain, she now and again even cracked a feeble joke; and, what was unfortunate, behaved much better than Ninian, who was all but beside himself. He who had been so patient with her querulousness in Madrid was infuriated by her composure in their present awful pass; he who had so criticized her failure to value the qualities of Spain found her more tolerant of the defects than he, admirer, expounder and furnisher of copious Iberian footnotes. Angrily he told himself that but for her cowardice they would by now be lying on the sunny beach at La Cabeza, listening to the splash of the waves or the occasional gruff speech of fishermen: he reminded himself that she was far younger and more resilient, he formulated a doctrine that women were all less developed and cruder than men and accordingly felt everything less; but do what he might he could not deny that she was showing herself here the better fellow, and he could not forgive her.

His anger persisted when the nightmare at last was at an end and, rested, bathed, restored, they sat at dinner in Málaga's most comfortable hotel. Never, he thought, had he seen her look as really awful as now, in the tight black satin dress run hastily up for her by Mrs Bernstein and with the huge coral earrings that belonged to Mumsie screwed onto her ears. She tried to woo him, saying how delightful it all was, how charming Málaga appeared to be, how lovely to be warm again, why, look, all the windows were open and those yellow things hanging on the tree outside must surely be oranges; but he would have none of it.

"Thirty years ago this country was worth seeing," he said glumly, closing it to her once and for all.

Gradually they left off talking to each other and finished their meal in silence: almost at once they went to their beds with only a brief "good night."

He had a curious dream, of being driven in a lorry by Mrs Bentley towards the cliff of the Cheddar Gorge. As she drove she entertained him with stories of the pranks she and her friend had played on some hapless guest at a country house, the itching powder slipped into his underpants, the powder dissolved in his drink that brought about such side-splitting physiological results, the ingenious exploits with rolls of lavatory paper. More than once he tactfully attempted to warn her of the approaching abyss but, laughing merrily, she paid no attention until at the very last, with a screech of "Tally ho!" she sprang from the lorry and left him to his fate.

It was not the dream itself that was curious, for Mrs Bentley had in truth regaled him with such memoirs early on in their acquaintance, and it was his lack of real appreciation which had first revealed to her that, besides having no sense of humour, he could not be quite out of the top drawer. No, the strange part of it was the emotion that the dream aroused, the definite pleasure that Mrs Bentley was speaking to him again, the sense of a burden being lifted; and on waking, once the relief of not being flung down the Cheddar Gorge was over, a real inexplicable disappointment that it had only been a dream. That really was strange, that really could not be understood; and as he lay thinking it over all at once a picture of Silverwood in the winter sun, the trees bare, the lake the colour of steel, the grass and stone all coated with frost, rose before his mind's eye and he thought to himself, I shall be glad enough to go back there.

Fifteen

After breakfast Mr La Touche dictated one or two letters to Miss Fellowe. These letters were never posted, were no more than a ritual carried out in the hope of establishing some contact at least with the ground, for he had all at once a nightmarish sense as of their being together in a rogue balloon that danced giddily here and there over tantalizingly familiar landscapes. Miss Fellowe was a little taken aback, as she had assumed that this phase of their association was now at an end; and she was even more surprised to find after a while that she was enjoying it. As Ninian disintegrated before her eyes in the train, turning from her rich, wise admirer into a peevish old man with baggy eyes and sour breath, she had become aware for the first time that age was not all serenity, poise and wealth, that there might even be worse things than youth and poverty and a drunken commercial-traveller father. She had been stabbed by a sudden realization that one day she would be old herself and, unless she turned out a good deal cuter than she felt, would not even be rich. These intimations had been about the last straw on the load of the day's misery, and it was a comfort this morning to see Ninian kindly, aloof and paternal again, as she had always liked him to be.

"How many times must I tell you there is no T in Richard?" he asked, frowning over a letter to Reynolds. "If you put one in again, you shall stand in the corner."

At the note of teasing authority in his voice she felt her flagging interest in him revive a little. He corrected all the letters with prodigious care, signed them, folded them into envelopes and forgot all about them immediately.

Ninian continued in her good books by making the plans for their day without consulting her. As the weather was so fine they would, like good tourists, drive round the town and the Alameda in one of the ancient buggies waiting near the port: they would lunch at a delightful restaurant on the beach—if it were still there, for he had not been to Málaga for six years and nowadays things changed overnight; and after the siesta would go every yard of the way, cost what it would, to La Cabeza by taxi.

"No more trains or coaches," he said. "Spain can hardly have any shots left in her locker, but we are not going to give her a chance."

It was a day of glowing sunshine, warm as an English May, and not at all suited to an elegant red coat with an astrakhan collar. Mercy saw nothing for it but to put on her old terylene suit, whose shabby youthful appearance she tried to mitigate by a liberal dressing of the mauve lipstick Mrs Bernstein had advocated. Ninian raised an eyebrow as she came into the hall.

"What in the name of goodness have you smeared on your face, little Hottentot?" he asked. "Go and take it off this minute—and look sharp."

She tore contentedly upstairs and took it off. Ninian found himself warming to her again as well, with her puppyish obedience and gusto, wearing the dreadful little grey jacket she had worn when he saw her for the first time; and in warming to her he lost for a time the feeling of degradation that afflicted him. As the carriage stopped on the brow of a hill for them to enjoy the splendid panorama, the sparkling sea with its fringe of trees, the blue peaks and smoky olive-clad foothills of the Morenas to the south and the mighty snowcapped Sierras far away in the north, a dreamy look came over her face; and when, half-hoping to hear something fresh or vivid enough to justify a little his former opinion, he asked what she was thinking about she answered, "Leo Piper," a reply so characteristic in its utter irrelevance that it delighted him.

As if vexed by Ninian's believing that her ammunition could ever run out, Spain saw to it that their taxi broke down in the middle of Torremolinos. They had to wait for an hour and a half while the driver, in leisurely style and with frequent pauses for discussion, argument and *copitas* with colleagues, diagnosed the trouble and set it right. Ninian took Mercy to a café in the square while the men bent over the leaky petrol tank with lighted cigars in their mouths: it was the kind of thing he never quite got used to.

"Only a few years ago this was a tiny fishing village, like the one we're going to," he said. "And just look at it now!"

"I think it's lovely," she said, looking at the row of gift shops with rapture.

"Oh! Well, we can come here if you find La Cabeza too quiet." To pass the time he told her about the village, the great rock like a man's head that gave it its name, the clean beaches and pure sea, the gentle hills behind that were covered with wild flowers and sweet herbs, the fisherfolk simple and dignified. Many of those he had known would now be dead. On clear days they would see the coast of Africa, and beyond it the towering bulk of the Atlas range that had so fired his imagination as a boy. And he had never returned to La Cabeza since that time, but kept it as a memory too precious to risk spoiling.

Mercy listened to him politely, with her eyes on the gift shops, and the thousand women flitting to and fro.

Their taxi drove up, the driver angrily shouting that they must be gone, as if the whole delay had been some vexatious caprice of their own. The reek of petrol filled the car as they bumped at a furious pace down the winding coast. After a time the driver yelled over his shoulder to ask what part La Cabeza he should take them to.

"To the inn," said Ninian.

"*To the inn!* Hombre! Which 'inn'?"

He had a sudden terrible foreboding. "Is there more than one?" he asked nervously.

The driver turned right round in his seat, oblivious of all but his wish to get a look at this fool of a stranger. "There are fifty!" he shouted. "Or maybe a hundred." Turning forward again, he took both hands off the wheel and lit a cigar. "And they are not inns, they are lujo hotels." The appalled face of his client mollified him, and he continued more cheerfully, "The Costa del Sol, Señor, develops from day to day. Take La Cabeza! Ten years ago a primitive settlement of hunger and poverty. Today, not only hotels, but private villas of every description, as far as the eye can see. There are campings, for the caravan. Nightclubs there are, bars, shops, and a plage. Very soon Torremolinos will be left behind."

"Oh, my God!"

"What's the matter? What is he saying?" Mercy wanted to know.

"It seems that La Cabeza has changed since my day," he told her heavily. "It is catching up with Torremolinos." How could I be so utterly inane as not to find out? he wondered.

"Ooh, Ninny! How lovely!"

In his national pride the driver had overstated the number of hotels. There were but seven, great jerry-built barns with glaring neon lights, and three more under construction. The private villas, however, did extend as far as the eye could see and were of every fantastic shape that tasteless ingenuity could devise. Why, Ninian pondered, do the rising bourgeoisie want things to look like other things: why had a house to look like a ship or a beehive, why must a garden stool resemble a mushroom? And why too, he wondered as with eyes starting from his head he took in one hideous erection after another, had he imagined this harsh awkward Spain that he loved to be immune from the urban vulgarity creeping over all Europe like a blight? Good heavens, she surpassed them all! Not the south of France, not the coast of Belgium, could show anything like it. And under it all were buried, like the wild flowers and the aromatic scrub, some of the happiest recollections of his youth.

"Oh, Ninny, isn't it *perfect?* I am so glad we came." Mercy was gazing at the great rock of La Cabeza, ingeniously flattened on top to make an open-air café with strings of multicoloured lights encircling it. "It's much nicer than Madrid."

"Let us settle down in one of those splendid hotels," he told her kindly, "and then we'll explore this beauty spot."

The driver insisted on their going to El Peru, a hotel on the seashore near some white fishermen's hovels that looked forlorn and redundant, like a settlement for decadent aborigines. It left all the others far behind for beauty, luxury and comfort, he assured them, it truly was *precioso* and a nephew of his worked in the kitchen. As he left them in the foyer, which was arranged to look like a clearing in the Amazonian forest with live parakeets and stuffed monkeys and snakes, he forgave them at last for the taxi having broken down, beamed upon them, repeatedly shook hands with Ninian and admired the

Señora's beauty. The receptionist booked them in without irony or disapproval, and was hardly dissuaded from putting them in one room: La Cabeza plainly took these little things in its stride.

An immense weariness overcame Ninian when the matter of the rooms was finally settled. He was stiff and sore from their terrible journey from Madrid, his head ached after the rigours of the taxi ride from Málaga and with the shock of La Cabeza's transfiguration the last little prop he had was kicked away. Spain has shot her bolt now, she really must have, he told himself as he went to the bathroom to bathe his dusty face and aching eyes. There was no water in the taps, and he seemed to catch, faintly, far away, a burst of demon laughter. It was over now and done with, all the nonsense: he should do what he could to see that Mercy enjoyed herself in this inferno, pleasure in the pleasure of the young being the only one seemly for an old man. Then home, and peace.

It was the hour of the *aperitivo,* when the cream of Cabezan society gathered in the bar El Mono Destacado. English, Dutch, American, German, bohemians, gigolos, crooks, old women on the spree, rich young men pretending to be artists, poor young men posing as writers, catamites, abusive middle-aged lovers, trollops with greasy hair and dirty hands—Ninian thought he had never seen such a collection in his life. The waiter told him that many of them had moved over from Tangier after Moroccan independence, and was surprised at Ninian's surprise: he clearly believed all foreigners everywhere were like his customers.

"They bring out the prig in me, I confess," Ninian said.

"I think they all look very interesting," Mercy said. "Unusual. I'll bet a lot of them are celebrated."

"Then I shan't be able to let you out of my sight," he mocked at her. "Or you'll be making unsuitable acquaintances. There's a delightfully grubby young gentleman staring at you now."

"He's staring at you, not me."

The grubby young gentleman now rose and made his way across the room to their table. He was dressed in a workman's overalls, but did not look like a man who worked. "Say, you don't have to tell me who you are," he drawled. "And why don't you have to tell me who you are. Because I know. You're Poppy's brother!"

"Half-brother," Ninian said automatically.

"Is that so?" The young man peered into his face. "Why you're the spit an' image of her. Give Poppy a beard and you could be twins?" He turned round and called to the little group he had been sitting with, "Hey! Duke! Mandy! Pearl! Come on over, folks. Here's Poppy's brother!"

"Half-brother," Ninian said. His mind had all but stopped functioning.

The trousered girls and unkempt youths rose all together like starlings and fluttered joyously about his table. Why, for land's sake! they chattered. Well, what do you know? We heard about you! How was it in gaol? Is this the girl friend? The words "Poppy's brother" flashed round the room with the speed of light and Ninian became a focal point of interest.

"Too bad you missed her," his tormentor proceeded. His name seemed to be Richmond. "She was here till, why, just four days ago, and she planned on going on to stay with some rich guy near Salamanca that's a marquis?" He had a trick of raising his voice interrogatively at the end of statements and dropping it at the end of questions. "Then she got this bad noos from home and she had to beat it?"

"Bad news?" echoed Ninian dully: as if anything connected with Mrs Cloud could be anything else.

"Yeah," Richmond said. "She didn't wanna say what it was, but it sure was bad. I never saw a dame as mad before, and I seen plenty mad dames?"

Duke intervened to say *he'd* seen plenty mad dames and *he* never saw a dame as mad. They all sat down, looking at Ninian and Mercy with affectionate interest, and Richmond waved his arms at the waiter. That experienced man gave Ninian a sardonic glance as he came up.

"I guess we'll all have Fundador," Richmond said in his slow way. "It's the most alcoholic content for the money? Say, Pearl, why isn't Dora here."

"Ow, don't you know?" Pearl said in a cockney accent, her thin face lighting up. "She's gone to Paris for a nabortion."

"Gee! Paris, France?"

"Well, it isn't in Turkey. Fancy going all that way! But they're s'pposed to be very partikklar here. And it fits in, they were going to put her out of the Casa Blanca for setting it on fire."

"Why didn't she go to Sweden?" Duke asked. "It's legal there. You can go in and have it done any place. It isn't breaking the law. She could have it on the level in Sweden."

"She wanted it on the cheap," Pearl explained.

"What's cheap about going to Paris, France?" Richmond appeared as anxious to get everything quite straight as Duke was to avoid ambiguity.

"She got a lift up there with this Baron," Pearl told him, "and she has these friends in the roo de la Paix."

"Gee."

"We all adored your sister," Mandy said. "Women of that age can be such hell. Poppy's a charming person."

"She's my half-sister," Ninian replied, looking at her, surprised to hear a lady's voice coming from the sluttish dissipated young woman before him. It somehow added to his distress, his sense of utter chaos. "She gets her enormous love of life from her mother's family. The Gurney exuberance was famous, even in the seventeenth century. Unhappily, Mrs Cloud's mother was the last of them."

"Really? I would have thought you were twins." She gave him a quizzical stare.

"Say, listen here, Poppy's brother," Richmond commanded. "Voo tombay a pick, as they say in Paris, France. I got a male gipsy dancer coming to my place tonight? Why don't you come on up, you and the girl friend."

"Miss Fellowe is my secretary," Ninian began, but his voice was drowned in laughter.

"Say, I didn't know anyone still played it that way," Richmond chuckled. "They mostly don't, around here!"

"We're all friends, love," Pearl said cosily. "No need for false shime."

214

"I don't know why the statement of a fact should result in this," Ninian said, pleasantly. "Miss Fellowe *is* my secretary."

"Sure! And I'm Mary Queen of Scots, though I don't tell everybody. And you've come to La Cabeza for peace and quiet, so's you can get some work done?" Richmond smiled at him lazily. "Okay. But listen! Don't you and your stenographer want to come on up and see this male gipsy dancer."

"Ooh, Ninny, do let us!" the stenographer cried, raising another good laugh.

"You go by all means, my dear. I have a lot of things to see to."

"Hell, no," Richmond said. It seemed that he would be unable to fix the stenographer up with a boy at such short notice, and fixed up with a boy she must be if she were not to feel entirely out of it? Poppy's brother wouldn't want his stenographer to feel entirely out of it. He'd forget the boss and act the boy friend just one little time. Ninian saw that the boss and the stenographer was going to be one of those jokes that shy or resentful people work to death. He argued for a little, then feebly gave in; and the six of them set off with farewells screamed at them from all over the café, to Richmond's house. This, the Casa Terrible as he called it, was a large and repulsively furnished villa a few yards above the old white parish church.

The male gipsy dancer had not arrived, although the furniture at one end of the room had been pushed back to the wall in readiness. On a table at the other end was the remains of Richmond's lunch and breakfast. Some garments were hanging out on a line suspended from corner to corner. Richmond poured out beakers of Fundador as if it were beer, and passed them round before embarking on an easy, informal line of talk that filled Ninian with amazement. To rebel against his own decorous environment was one thing, to thumb his nose at the Bench, to play the little madcap with Mrs Bentley: but now, strayed into the real world of abandoned youth, he became just an analysing, annotating old fogy. These young people had nothing at all in their heads but their sexual adventures, which they discussed with a fantastic solemnity: from their grave intent faces and level tone of voice they might have been young communists threshing out a new three-year plan for the collective.

"Sarah was on the beach again, having one of those Spanish fishing boys?" Richmond drawled. "Is that dame crazy. Doctors told her, next time she gets pneumonia it's curtains? I figure that dame is crazy." But even the medical aspect of Sarah's behaviour aroused no real disapprobation.

"There's Milly Duval wearing herself out looking for a man to keep her," Pearl remarked, with a shake of the head. "I said, 'Look 'ere, dearie, face fax. Would you pay for something that you can have it for free?' She says, 'Pearl, no man can't have me for free.' I says to her straight, 'Not *you*, dearie,' I says, 'but fourteen others eggzackly like you.' She can't see it."

"Why, I always thought Milly had money," ruminated Duke. "That girl looks to me like a moneyed girl. I'd have said, that girl's a girl with money."

"So she is," Mandy said, "but she would not be averse to have some more."

Presently the conversation took a literary turn. La Cabeza had newly been visited by a brilliant young English novelist who ran the fornications and adulteries of his engrossing heroes, provincial shop assistants as a rule, into more hundreds of pages than anyone would have thought feasible. The red carpet had of course been laid for this powerful thinker, but what had tickled La Cabeza pink was the report of various local beauties, each claiming to know, that his own apparatus was all but invisible to the human eye without artificial aid, and with a performance to match. This reminded Mandy of poor dear D. H. Lawrence, and poor dear D.H.L. reminded Duke of Mexico, which switched them all to tequila and the fact that their beakers were dry; and Richmond opened another bottle of Fundador.

An hour later the male gipsy dancer had not arrived and Richmond said, "Hell, maybe the guy isn't gonna come." He poured out some Fundador. Time went on passing.

Am I getting drunk? Ninian wondered, swallowing this liquid with the odd taste of burnt sugar. There was a straining and jarring and throbbing in his head as if the engines of a ship had been fitted there, but the deadly fatigue was all gone. Mercy looked flushed and happy, quite at her ease and prettier than he had ever known her. Of course not, he answered his own question: I was never drunk in my life and therefore cannot be now. But he had never drunk neat Spanish brandy in his life. He turned away from the company

217

and looked out through a window behind him at the sea, at the blades of garish light plunged into the unprotesting water round La Cabeza, beyond them at the dark oily surface sparkling only here and there with a touch of moon or star. "The moon doth with delight look round her when the heavens are bare; waters on a starry night are beautiful and fair. But yet I know, where'er I go . . ." His heart came into his mouth then, even as it had done at the entrance to the wood that day not so very long, and yet ages, ago; and to the surprise of the company he leaped to his feet, sending his chair to the floor with a crash.

"It is absurd! It is ridiculous!" he cried, stammering in his passion. "Why has no one ever ruined the sea?"

"Okay, Pop, you wanna take it easy?" Richmond withdrew an arm from Pearl's waist and exchanged a glance with Duke.

"Hundreds and miles of virgin sea all over the globe," Ninian babbled, "crying out, crying out to be raped, developed, despoiled and ruined! Is it beyond the ingenuity of man? There should be coloured lights everywhere along the waterways of the world . . . there should be night clubs, juke boxes, information bureaux . . ."

"Say listen here, Pop," said the humane host, "what you say I cut you a bocadillo with sausage and pan moreno. Duke, oughn't Pop have a bocadillo with sausage and pan moreno."

"What Pop needs right now," Duke heartily affirmed, "is a bocadillo with sausage and pan moreno."

"Are you young men inshin . . . niswin . . . suggesting that I am drunk?" Ninian's rage mounted

218

with every second. "Simply because I happen to feel that the sea should be developed as a resort?" He realized, none the less, that he must take hold of himself, if he were not to say something foolish. "If you don't mind I shall go back to my hotel," he said, cool and dignified. "Tomorrow I have to go looking for some abstract painters."

"Why, that's swell, Pop, you go on home and get some rest," they said. Richmond asked if he wanted a taxi and Ninian replied that the walk and the fresh air would do him good. "But you might get one for Miss Fellowe in due course, if you will," he requested, admiring his own clear speech and orderly ideas. "And thank you for a very pleasant evening."

"Why, you're certainly welcome, Poppy's brother. Too bad about that male gipsy dancer."

They courteously walked to the door and shut it after him. The effect on Ninian of passing from the bright light to semidarkness was appalling: immediately there was nothing for his eyes to focus on and cling to, the ship's engine inside his head was transformed into an aeroplane's propeller that revved up faster and faster in a mad race to get him off the ground. He reeled to and fro in despair, knowing the battle was lost, until with a loud dreadful cry he fell to earth.

Richmond opened the door again and said, "Gee." He and Duke brought a stretcher that leaned against the wall in readiness for contingencies of the kind, and together, with a kind of antlike concentration and method, they lifted Ninian up and laid him on it. Robbed of all power, yet still vaguely observing his environment, he noted that it was a real hospital stretcher and thought after all what sensible capable boys they were. He noticed too that they had the same grave, intent, unjudging air about them now as when they talked of the capers of themselves and their friends.

One thing, there's no need ever to feel embarrassment with this generation, he reflected, thinking of the shamefaced apologies of the old Admiral after one of his little collapses.

The young men raised the litter and steered it through the lemon trees in the garden to the stony ill-lit road. Mercy was saying confidentially to Pearl, "I liked him really better when he was Mr La Touche." He was puzzled by this remark of hers because he was Mr La Touche, was he not? He rather believed he was. The clouds slipped away from the moon and a glittering silver arm was thrown eagerly round the sea. "The moon doth with delight . . ." He would put Silverwood on the market at once and go to live in Cornwall, on the farthest wave-lashed tip of rocky coast. But there was no time, no time, no time. Did old Tally ho ever feel the icy breath of terror in the watches of the night? Not she. In his whirling mind the image of a peony-red face on a pillow followed that of himself as he crouched on his Cornish rock. Now as the boys bore him rythmically along with the ease of long practice he saw that women knelt in the road as he passed them by, crossing themselves and murmuring in prayer. They think I am dying or dead, he thought. The idea pleased him very much, as much as if he had deliberately tried to fox them. He wished to acknowledge and salute their devotion by taking off his hat, for like many scoffers and unbelievers he always displayed an exaggerated reverence for the pieties of others; but his hat was not on his head, or at least he could not find it there. Where, then, was it? When last had he had it? In Madrid? Someone was intoning now, people were chanting responses in unison, there was a flicker of candlelight, a whiff of incense. With disappointment he saw that it was not for him the women knelt, but for a real corpse that was being carried up to lie overnight in the church. Two acolytes led the procession, a burly Franciscan with a long white beard following them, then came the lighted bier, then a group of sorrowing women, like old black-hooded crows. One of these mourners was the image of Violet. We must have Spanish blood in us, Ninian told himself, pleased with this idea as well. All at once he found something exquisitely comic in the whole affair, why he could not have said, but the bodies passing each other silently on the darkened road, the dead going to Holy Church, the quick to El Peru, it was divinely funny. "I'm in hell, in El, Peru," he sang and burst out laughing. An acolyte furiously rang his bell and the old friar shouted something about foreigners and blasphemers.

"Wanna take it easy, Pop?" Richmond said without emotion.

When the funeral cortege had gone there was another little contretemps but by now he was too drowsy to take it in completely. It seemed that Mandy fell into a vast hole that the Spaniards had dug for purposes of their own and then neglected to rail off or illumine. She lay at the bottom of this pit screaming, he rather imagined, that there were serpents crawling over her. But he was fast leaving the turbulent world of thought and feeling and episode. There was a last little glimpse of the trembling, moonstruck sea and he quietly passed out. Duke and Richmond carried the unconscious figure steadily into El Peru and laid it, under the dispassionate eye of the *conserje de noche,* among the parrots, monkeys, snakes and gaudy blooms of the Amazonian jungle.

Sixteen

"My love, Miss La Touche is not quite the thing," said Dr Benn to his wife a week before Christmas. "Would you take on the kiddies' party for her?"

Mrs Benn had studied the doctor's idiom for many years and she looked at him in distress. "Oh, I am sorry, Horatio, very sorry indeed," she said. "Yes, I will do the party. Of course, we haven't the Silverwood space. But we'll manage the best we can."

"The parson will give us the parish hall," he continued. "You couldn't possibly do the youngsters' hop as well, if we all bear a hand?"

Mrs Benn laid her knitting down and looked at him once more, with tears in her eyes. "Of course I will," she said, and slowly took her knitting up again.

"That's my Birdie," and he bustled away to tele-phone and tell Violet about the new arrangements which, he said, were doctor's orders.

"You are most terribly kind to me," Violet said, aware of the sacrifice the doctor was making. Christ-mas was a time of anguish for him, when he could go nowhere without seeing pile upon pile of candied fruits, grinning boars' heads, huge turkeys, barons of beef, cakes lethally almond-pasted and sugar-iced, all the fearful means by which the humanity of which he remained so obstinately fond sought to achieve its frantic desire for premature death. He liked to spend the whole period quietly at home, out of sight, feast-ing upon an apple or two and a few assorted nuts, lying *perdu* until the telephone should ring and give details of the first casualty. Instead, and for her sake, he was actually prepared to connive at and partici-pate in the whole insane, criminal, suicidal, savage, tribal procedure! She was greatly moved and, once the burden was taken from her, realized how very heavy it would have been.

"Nonsense!" he barked at her in the peppery tone he used when people tried to thank him. "And do try and relax!"

Ah, yes, to be sure, Violet thought. She was less re-laxed and more unhappy at this time than ever be-fore. Her loneliness had all at once grown unbeara-ble, partly because two delightful things had come about and there was no one to enjoy them with her.

First, as she was reading the popular press as usual one morning, her eye had been caught by the name of William Box. The distinguished conductor had been making for St James's Park with a bag of crumbs for the waterfowl there, prior to holding a concert of Hindemith, Schönberg and Shostakovich at the Festival Hall, when all at once he had been assailed by five individuals, of whom the leader was a woman, who attempted to overpower him and drag him into a car that waited nearby with the engine running. Mr Box defended himself with great valour, holding his assailants off until a number of soldiers in Wellington Barracks came racing out to bring their help. The miscreants were apprehended and charged and turned out, to the general amazement, to be no common hooligans or thieves but a Major Nightingale, the Professors Meyerbach and Fothergill, and the Doctors Mallock and Gamgee, all of the Oxford Foundation for Experimental Physiological Research. Mr Box could think of no explanation of the attack and vehemently denied that it was in any way connected with actions of his own. He pointed out that if everyone were to behave like that, our civilization would come to an end. The four scientists were bound to the peace but Major Nightingale was heavily fined, inquiries at Oxford having shown that only a week before she had, single-handed, thrown two of the Foundation's male employees over Magdalen Bridge, on the grounds of their having passed secrets to the enemy.

Hardly had Violet finished smiling over this than she thought with an ache in her heart how Ninian would have relished it all, how edified he would have been to hear that four brilliant scientists and a lady of military experience had been worsted by one batty musician, and how delighted by the further revelation of Billy's unplumbable depths of depravity; for that slippery customer had always denied using agents within the Foundation and claimed to know all it did by a peculiar marvellous intuition. There was not even an address to which the cutting might be sent. And if Ninian would have loved this story, what would he not have said to the case of Olimpia? A case so beautiful, right and awe-inspiring as to make Violet wonder if after all some Mighty Hand were not benevolently guiding and ruling the universe.

As the cold wet winter settled in, Desdemona took a chill and could not throw it off. She lay in her little cot, trembling and whispering to herself with her skinny arms folded across her tiny chest, and rejected food, caresses and consolation of every kind. Violet noticed one day that Olimpia now constantly wore a garment like a mauve dressing gown with a yellow cord round the waist, the outward sign, Tito explained, of a private agreement she had entered into with Santa Maria Goretti. She had taken a solemn vow to do something or other, should the saint be able to arrange for Desdemona's recovery; although she might not reveal what that vow was until affairs were regulated in one way or another.

After a time of dreadful suspense the little monkey passed away; and Olimpia's sorrow was equalled only by her rage at the Goretti's incompetence. She should have known better, she shrieked, than to entrust so delicate a business to a *bimba* like that, a chit of a girl who had not been canonized long enough to know her way round. And she, Olimpia, had been prepared to visit the Saint's birthplace on foot! From the nearest railway station. She, Olimpia Ricci, who never walked to the garden for a sprig of parsley if she could help it! Ah, but Olimpia Ricci was not the woman to take an affront lying down. Olimpia Ricci was no one's plaything, no, let them be a thousand times saint. Now, to punish the Goretti and teach her a lesson, she took another solemn vow, never, never to cook again for the rest of her mortal span, never again to put pot to fire or tray to oven while yet she lived and breathed.

"Will she keep to it, Tito?" Violet demanded. There was something of the remorseless sweep of Greek drama in these events. Manley was entirely committed. So fearful was he lest the cup be dashed from his lips in spite of all that he had actually had a contract drawn up with the Italians, by which both sides were bound to each other; but in his greedy haste and his *hubris* he had omitted to specify what duties were assigned to which party, and Tito was a perfectly good plain cook.

"Oh, the Olimpia never break the *parola,*" the little man proudly answered, pressing both hands to his heart. "I think maybe two-a, t'ree-a year before she cook again."

Violet had sighed with pleasure, for even two years of simple wholesome food would cast a long shadow over the historian's life.

So there was that, and there was Billy, and Ninian was not there to laugh with her. He was fooling about in the south of Spain with his typist, pretending to be twenty again. The fact that things were taking a turn for the better, were arranging themselves all at once, at Silverwood only made her desolation the more complete. Even the doctor's kindness merely rubbed in the pain of her brother's indifference. The Riccis had fished up from among their innumerable kinsmen a married couple who wanted to work in England. Mr Isolowolotumba wrote to put off his visit, explaining with African sincerity that he had another invitation from somebody more important. Life was easing up all round, and even the weather had turned warm and sunny. Looking out of the window now, she saw the pearly glow of a Christmas rose among the bare dark shrubs. Every year she and Ninian watched for it at this time, hoping the plants would bloom for Christmas; and seeing the lovely little white and gold cup there she felt suddenly bitter against him.

Is he the only one who hates dying? she wondered.

And then, as if the fates had at last determined to relent, the afternoon post brought his letter. He was going back to Madrid almost at once to finish business there, before coming home early in the New Year. Mercy had made some young friends in La Cabeza and would spend Christmas with them, returning later by sea from Gibraltar. He hoped Violet was in good health as usual: he could not say as much for himself, and would have to see Benn about some disquieting new symptoms that had occurred since he left England. He would wire the day and time of his arrival at London airport in due course, and he was ever her loving Nin. He had not used the "Nin" to her for years; and there was a P.S., "I'm longing to get back."

She was still reading it and rereading it when all at once the room grew dim and smoky and resignedly she prepared to fall yet again into the black pit from which, she supposed, one of these days there would be no return. Instead, after a few moments the air became once more bright and clear as if even her mortal disease were intimidated by the changing mood of the gods. The drawing room ceased to be a blank in which one moved distractedly about thinking of other things and took on the old familiar look, the beloved treasures in it calling her attention to themselves one by one with an air of triumph. Presently she got up and went into the garden, visited the Christmas rose, watched McCardle wheel a heavy barrowload of straw across the lawn—once his pride and joy, to be unremittingly fed, watered, weeded, rolled, and walked on by nobody else—for the greater convenience and comfort of his ewes, now approaching the most beautiful experience in feminine life. On she walked, slowly, relishing the afternoon air, and paused by the sundial to get her breath, recollecting Miss Fellowe's serious little face as she proposed their putting the sun back, Ninian's wish that they only might; and suddenly found herself shaking with laughter, so that she could hardly go on her way. Everything caught her eye, everything was of interest, everything brought memories: she noted all about her as for many a week she had not done. The deodars did not appear to thrive, due possibly to McCardle's sabotage. A solitary oak in the wood had kept its leaves on and stood in a blaze of yellow among the skeletons all about it. Perhaps the lake had a fault in it, for the water appeared to be very low. Lists of things to be done formed themselves in her mind now that peace and tranquillity were coming back and her remaining years or months would be spent in monastic calm as she had always intended.

At teatime she notified the Siamese severally and as a group that henceforth they must keep to their own quarters. After dinner she played Ravel and Debussy on the piano that for so long had not been opened, and went early to bed. She took no drugs at all and slept dreamlessly until after nine in the morning, when she came downstairs greatly refreshed and with a sense of heightened well-being and recruited powers.

A horrifying spectacle met her eyes as she turned the bend in the stairway. Mrs Poppy Cloud was in the hall alone, pacing up and down with a tigerish tread that accorded ill with her fashionably balloon-like coat and pagoda hat. Catching sight of Violet, she raised one forefinger to her lips to enjoin silence and with the other stabbed in the direction of the servants' hall to explain the need for it: then, beckoning to her sister to follow, she tiptoed into the library, shut the door behind them, folded her arms and uttered the dire words: "My daughter, a fallen woman!"

"My good Poppy, what can you mean?" Violet spoke drily, for she disliked theatrical effects and was not at all in the mood for entertaining Mrs Cloud.

"What I say, Violet, what I say. My daughter, *a fallen woman!*" As if indeed she were some minor actress with but a single line in which to pour out and express her entire personality, she repeated this statement with varying emphasis: "My *daughter,* a fallen woman! *My* daughter, a fallen woman!"

"Do leave off, you are making my head spin. Sit down and tell me what has happened," and Violet wearily sat down herself.

"Seven months and more, gone with child!" Horror, amazement, grief were written all over Poppy's battleworn face. "My little Isabel! It seems only the other day . . ."

"And you've just tumbled to it now?"

"I have been much from home this year," Poppy said with dignity. "My many friends were complaining they saw so little of me. I trusted her, Violet. She always made out she was going to be a nun, the trollop. I was to have taken the veil myself, in a Zen Buddhist order, when she did so. I will never forgive her."

The Gurney blood again, thought Violet, but aloud she merely said, "Come now, what chance did the poor child ever have?"

Poppy's generous mouth hung open in sheer astonishment. "*What chance,* Violet? can you be serious?" she quavered, as soon as she had collected herself sufficiently to speak. "Educated at Le Petit Cœur de Jésus. Finished at Montreux. Her own account at Fortnum's. Her mother's constant companion whenever her mother had time. Living in the greatest comfort, refused nothing, a cocktail named after her when only fifteen . . ." Mrs Cloud was unable to go on, overwhelmed by so base a return for all these advantages.

"Who is responsible?" Violet asked, to avoid controversy.

"The baggage won't tell me," Poppy said indignantly. "She only says he is away. I have been through her correspondence and found nothing. She refuses to go abroad, as any self-respecting strumpet would. She hangs on in London, shaming me and making everyone laugh. She must have something against me, I can't imagine what."

"Your attitude surprises me a little," Violet said, with Mrs Cloud's own epoch-making career in mind. "I understand that any number of young people to-day have experiences before they marry."

"It is not so much the experience I object to," Poppy freely admitted. "It is the baby."

"One rather leads to the other," Violet disclosed. "It has even been held to be the purpose of the whole arrangement."

Mrs Cloud sniffed and drew herself up. "Not by our sort of people, my dear," she retorted. "And no one likes to be a grandmother before her time." There was a scream and a roar and a bang in the sky: the house trembled. "Violet! what on earth was that?"

"Some young gentleman has just broken the sound barrier."

"You don't mean you've got those things out here? So far from Russia?"

"We have indeed. And this fine weather brings them out like wasps." Violet was engaged in an inward conflict. The sound of the warplane, unheard for so long, was a reminder that the monastic evening calm she had been promising herself might not be easy to attain in the contemporary world. There might, also, be other things that mattered a great deal more. She thought of the young, unhappy girl, defiant, embittered, of her face that for all the Cloud and Gurney blood was so utterly, completely La Touche: Ninian and she had always cared very much for Isabel and would have seen more of her but for her redoubtable mother. It crossed Violet's mind that she would not presumably enter a convent now, thus inheriting Silverwood after all and in time passing it on perhaps to this unborn child: the thought gave her a wicked satisfaction, and, with a quick resolve, she renounced all hope of peace and quiet.

"Isabel must come here," she said, "and I will look after her."

Poppy had driven all the way from London through what she called the freezing dawn with this very end in view, and now affected to be quite over-come with gratitude and surprise. "You wouldn't, Violet? Would you?" she panted. "Would Ninian allow it? He never would!"

"The house is mine as much as his, although we never stress the fact," Violet replied, admirably firm. "In any case, Ninian is going through a broad-minded phase."

"Really?" Mrs Cloud was brightening wonderfully with every moment. "Would he have me to stay?"

"Not quite such a broad-minded phase as that."

"He has never understood me," Poppy lamented. "He has never *tried* to understand me. I have been a closed book to him, as a woman and as a person. Both as woman and as person," she repeated weight-ily. "And if I take up Zen he may never get the chance again. Think of it, Violet! We are none of us getting any younger. Ninian will regret this long estrangement when I am buried in some Japanese Buddhist temple."

"It will be no end of a Japanese Buddhist temple, I foretell," and, excusing herself, Violet went to the desk to write a warm affectionate invitation to her fallen niece. Poppy stowed the letter away, careful and reverent as a Queen's Messenger, with the lipstick, corkscrew, powder, gin flask, threatening correspondence, jolly-up tablets, calm-down tablets, spare set of teeth and booklet on the *Meaning of Non-Meaning,* by a Mr George Watanabe, in her handbag, and drove off in high feather. As Violet watched her go she felt simmering within her a variety of emotions wholly inappropriate to the present disgraceful state of affairs and such indeed as she could hardly remember ever experiencing before: a secret wicked mirth, a delightful anticipation, combined with joy for the child to be born in the house, happiness that she would play some little part in his coming and a persistent, disloyal, reprehensible hope that her brother would be unutterably shocked. Up to that moment, from the time when Mrs Cloud had broken her news, she had not really thought of him at all.

Ninian thought, In a quarter of an hour I shall see Violet. The Tower of London dangled above his head and the river was rearing up like a ladder as the aeroplane banked and stalled on the way down. Two Spaniards in the seat behind were complaining that there was no fog and no rain or anything *típico* or *clásico* at all. That evening there was only a great city under gathering blue mist with lights coming out one by one like stars: the romantic Spaniards would have to wait.

It was Ninian's real self who thus pleasurably looked forward to the reunion with his sister. Somewhere deep down a stifled voice was mourning and pleading but he firmly ignored it. The well-kept hand in the elegant glove grasped a rolled-up copy of *The Times* wherein, as a last little touch before the dossier was closed and filed, there was an account of the trial of Mr Piper. The jury having found him guilty and the tale of his previous mishaps having been read, his counsel made an impassioned plea for mercy on the grounds that Mr Piper had been starved of love all his life, could therefore not be blamed for thieving, forging, blackmailing, coshing and slashing and would only be embittered, not ennobled, by a long term in prison. His words moved all who heard them save the Judge. That unfeeling brute declared that nothing surprised him less than to hear that Mr Piper had not been a general favourite. He would go so far as to say he could not recall offhand any individual who had inspired him with a greater instinctive repugnance. Counsel would be astonished to learn, this horrid reactionary continued, that Mr Piper was not going to gaol to enrich, enhance and develop his interesting psyche but to be stopped from pillaging honest folk. Five years of preventive detention for Mr Piper, the Judge concluded with jovial sadism, would give Society time to get its breath. At that Mr Piper called for his mother, and two girls in the courtroom screamed and fainted.

Reading this, Ninian recollected one by one his own experiences with Mr Piper, which seemed now to have been those of someone else. Indeed, all that he had recently done now appeared to him as the act of a stranger, beyond his understanding. The one exception he made, the single little face-saver, was in the matter of Mercy Fellowe and the Dufy: he would still, and always, maintain that to have identified that painting at her age was a remarkable feat. The child was well worth a helping hand; and as soon as she returned from Spain he would send her to a good secretarial college.

But now they were landing and in due course the door was opened and, deafened and dazzled, the passengers went trickling down the gangway. To Ninian's surprise, Violet was nowhere to be seen. He had been careful to wire the date and hour because on another occasion he had omitted to do this and she had met every incoming plane for three days. He went to the message rack and there was nothing for him, the receptionist had received no word, there was no telegram. Mystified, he put in a call to Silverwood and after twenty minutes' delay was informed that the house was taking no calls, by subscriber's instructions.

"I am the subscriber," Ninian said. "Kindly put me through at once."

"Sorry, sir: subscriber's instruction."

"I am the subscriber."

"Sorry, sir: subscri—"

Ninian put the receiver down and telephoned to Reynolds, who could only say that Violet had rung him up the day before and had sounded particularly happy. From the eager friendliness of his junior partner's voice Ninian knew that word of his regained sanity had travelled already and that bygones were to be bygones; and he felt old and tired and sad.

"It is really not like Violet," he grumbled. "I expected her to be here with the car. How on earth am I to get home?"

"Could you not take the train?"

"My dear Dick!" Disappointment turned to vexation and ended in a fit of sulks. As Violet put herself out so little for him, he should spend the night in town and go on tomorrow at his leisure, without notifying her. Early next morning, however, refreshed by sleep and in a better mood, he began to fear that something had happened, that she might be ill, that those fainting spells were not after all due merely to feminine weakness or a desire for sympathy; and without breakfasting he hired a car to drive him home with all possible speed.

When at last he reached Silverwood the sight of Dr Benn's old jeep at the entrance made his pulses quicken with dread. He ought to have known, he thought with remorse, that one reason only could have kept his sister from meeting him, that sister who had been entirely and exclusively devoted to him from their childhood on. His suspicion of her neglect had been due to a guilty feeling that he deserved it, and he now tore up the steps without stopping even to think of the perilous strain on his heart.

As he ran into the hall, however, the first person he saw was Violet herself, hurrying downstairs with an air of purpose she seldom displayed. Furthermore, as she flashed by him with an abstracted "Ah, Nin, so you're back" he saw in her face the very same look, ardent and yet withdrawn, that Mary's had worn the day she sat up in bed and sketched. With amazement he watched her scuttle into the domestic interior and reappear, carrying a small bath with which she went staggering up the stairs again.

"Vi! Vi!" he called.

"Presently, presently," she panted without looking back.

The drawing-room door opened and Oliver Knox came out. "Oh, hullo," he said. "Thought I heard a car. Did you have a good trip?"

"What on earth is happening?" Ninian irritably inquired. He noticed that the great chandelier was shrouded in a dustcover and remembered with a pang that the Riccis were gone. With a childlike pleasure in its beauty Tito had always found time to keep it sparkling and glittering, and hanging there dead it was a cruel reminder of what they had lost. "Exactly what is going on?" he demanded.

"She left me," Oliver said with a tremor in his voice. "She ran away. I had no money, and Violet let me come here."

"I'm very sorry," Ninian said, trying to sound it. "I meant, what is going on in this house?"

"Oh, that," Oliver said. "Miss Cloud is having her baby."

"Miss Cloud? Isabel? *Her baby?*" Ninian stared blankly at the aggrieved face before him, experiencing again that odd sense of the world he knew dispersing and vanishing like a puff of smoke.

"Yes, poor girl. It is premature." But Oliver found it hard to fix his thoughts on anyone but himself. "Did you know there was madness in her family?" he asked.

"A little, perhaps, in the Gurneys." Ninian spoke automatically, in a stupor, and even as he uttered the words a jeering adenoidal voice began talking inside his brain. *Things run in families,* it said. *I'm sweet on Isabel. A nun? Isabel? That's rich!* "Oh, stop! Do stop!" he cried aloud.

"All right, no offence," Oliver said huffily. "I didn't mean the Gurneys, I meant the Taplins. There must be lunacy somewhere. How else can you explain her conduct?"

"That is what everyone said when she married," Ninian said distractedly, without being in the least aware of the puckering of Oliver's already lemon-sour face. He put a shaking hand to his brow. *I'm sweet on Isabel* . . . But she couldn't, she couldn't, she couldn't: quiet, fastidious little Isabel could never have . . . He found himself unable even to formulate the thought precisely. "When did this all begin?" he demanded. "Please tell me everything."

"Yesterday." Oliver drew himself up and spoke in the most freezing tone he could manage, to convey that only the fact of his being a guest induced him to reply at all. "After breakfast. She was reading the paper when suddenly she gave a cry and turned faint. The pains came on a few hours afterwards."

One of the silver monsters screamed through the air and banged. The familiar spirits were out and about. Ninian walked off to the library with slow dragging steps. *Things run in families. . . .* With fumbling elderly movements he lifted a decanter of cognac from the tray and made to pour himself a drink. Very gently it was taken from him and he turned, to find Violet at his elbow. He was touched by what he took to be solicitude for him but in the next moment perceived that she had still her aloof and dedicated air, and merely wanted the cognac for somebody else.

239

"Is she dying, Violet?"

"No, no. This is for Mrs Dimble." Violet was already flitting towards the door, decanter in hand. "Take Oliver for a walk, do," she requested as she ran. "Both of you keep out of the way."

"I want food!" he exclaimed loudly, stung by this attitude. His predominance in their joint lives was suddenly gone, he was to be paired with Knox as a male encumbrance, nothing apparently existed for Violet but the wanton Isabel and her brat. "I want breakfast—or lunch!" he grizzled.

"Ninian wants to be born too!" Violet teased him, and was gone.

He had forgotten the hired car, which now hooted impatiently for notice. As he went through the hall Oliver called out, "Don't you think she might have left me some money? There was not a penny in the house." Ninian began to think that all this might be a dream. When he had paid the driver and sent him off he stood in the sunshine looking at the familiar scene all round him in a daze. Everything was the same, yet everything looked strange. All the Christmas roses were in bloom. The lawn had a lived-on appearance, as if trippers had spent a Bank Holiday there. Very high up a lot of tiny planes were nosing methodically about the sky like tractors working a vast blue field. Not a cloud in sight: why then, the sound of falling rain? Then he realized that it was not rain but the gentle pattering of the ewes' feet as McCardle ushered them to the lawn for their daily browse. So they were still there, it was really beyond everything. How lax Violet had become! One, two, three, four . . . good heavens, they had lambed, abundantly, by twos and threes, and it was a whole thriving, frisking, tail-shaking little flock that trotted demurely behind their shepherd. At the fulfilled expression on McCardle's craggy face Ninian became aware of a kind of hilarity rising within him, mingled with a new excitement and a great wish to know how things were going in the house. He hastened back into the hall and said to Oliver, still loitering in it with a moonstruck air, "Where is she?"

"Not so much as a postcard from her," Oliver whined. "Just a note on the kitchen table, saying she painted better on her own."

Ninian wasted no more breath on the unlucky wight but hurried upstairs, pausing at the top and straining his ears. Voices came faintly from the bedroom next to Violet's own and with pounding heart he crept towards it until abruptly halted by the sound of a little feeble wavering howl, followed by a loud, merry laugh from Dr Benn. A wild, absurd happiness rushed over him then, a strange exultation and a feeling of the sweetness of life which would persist although he told himself that the circumstances hardly called for it. The terrible facts of the case seemed to fade from his mind as he stood there, smiling, savouring his misbegotten joy, until the door opened and Dr Benn came out, fresh as paint after his long night's work.

"Ha! Eavesdropping," he chuckled. "Adolescent curiosity. Congratulations on your great-niece. She has two of everything she ought to have two of. Miss La Touche and Mrs Dimble combined make a famous midwife. And the little mother is doing capitally. Bless me, the young people nowadays!"

"It is really too shocking for words," Ninian said happily.

"Can't think why you look so pleased, your nose is properly out of joint, my boy," the little doctor remarked with glee as they walked down the passage together. "No sane woman can think of anything else with a baby about. Come to that, we're not much different ourselves. And as times goes on we have to warm our hands at younger fires. The beard is off, I see. Too many mice in it?"

"Are you still writing your play?" Ninian countered in self-defence.

Dr Benn stiffened. "One day, La Touche, I shall surprise you all," he said quietly.

"No doubt of it. But I hardly expect to feel surprised again for a while."

"No, you looked forward to another kind of homecoming altogether," the doctor said, visibly cheered by the thought. "Red carpet stuff! But don't go cramming yourself with food to compensate for this trauma. Miss Cloud has a fine little girl," he called to Oliver as they reached the foot of the stairs, unable to conceive that anyone should not be passionately interested in so delightful a thing.

"One more woman! Oh, my God," was all the reply he got, and Oliver slunk away to the drawing room for a game of Patience.

"Warped," was the doctor's comment. "It must be the effect of living with his wife's pictures. Well, I'm away. Look after Miss La Touche for all you're worth, I do seriously beg of you."

"I rather want to have a talk with you about myself," Ninian began, but the doctor smiled and held out his hand in unmistakable valediction.

"I've promised you, you'll bury us all if you keep off the kedgeree," he assured him. He stowed his capacious bag in the rear of the jeep and was about to vault into it as usual when he suddenly thought better of it and opened the door. " 'The years like great black oxen tread the world,' " he said ruefully, getting in. "That's poetry, La Touche. I found it in a Christmas cracker. Airy-fairy. Give me," the little man said earnestly, "something I can get my teeth into. Maugham or Bridie. Every time." He started the engine. "Bye-bye!" he chirruped. "I hear Mrs Bentley has ruled that 'bye-bye' is common. Bye-bye!" And he drove off, singing, while Ninian went to the kitchen to cut some bread and cheese and to tell himself over and over again, without effect, how dire a catastrophe had befallen them all.

ABOUT THE AUTHOR

HONOR TRACY began writing in Dublin after the war, and toiled and starved in a conventional manner. Then for a time she did newspaper work and travelled over Europe and the Far East as a foreign correspondent. Her first book, *Kakemono: A Sketchbook of Postwar Japan,* was published in 1950. Since then she has written two other travel books, an Irish one, *Mind You, I've Said Nothing!,* and one on Spain, *Silk Hats and No Breakfast.*

Her works of fiction are *The Deserters, The Straight and Narrow Path*—a modern classic—*The Prospects Are Pleasing* and *A Number of Things.*

She lives on top of a hill near Dublin and travels whenever she can: apart from this and reading, her favorite occupation at present is growing flowers.

SOUTHERN PINES PUBLIC LIBRARY

3 8788 1002 9783 3

DATE

AUG 16 '69

AUG 2 '69

69

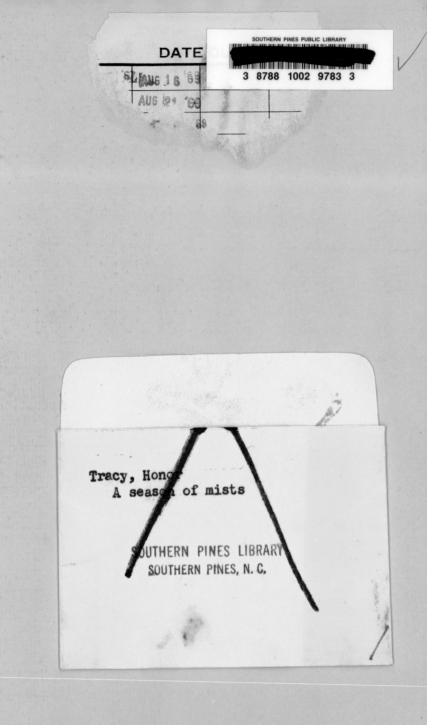

Tracy, Honor
A season of mists

SOUTHERN PINES LIBRARY
SOUTHERN PINES, N. C.